Bethel Library Assoc.
P.O. BOX 67
BETHEL, MAINE 04217

THE DROWNING SEASON

Bethel Library Assoc.
P. O. BOX 67
BETHEL, MAINE 04217

BY ALICE HOFFMAN

Property Of

THE DROWNING

E. P. Dutton • New York

SEASON

Alice Hoffman

Copyright © 1979 by Alice Hoffman • All rights reserved. Printed in the U.S.A. • No part of this publication may be reproduced or transmitted in any form or by any means, electronic or mechanical, including photocopy, recording or any information storage and retrieval system now known or to be invented, without permission in writing from the publisher, except by a reviewer who wishes to quote brief passages in connection with a review written for inclusion in a magazine, newspaper or broadcast • *For information contact: E. P. Dutton, 2 Park Avenue, New York, N.Y. 10016 • Library of Congress Cataloging in Publication Data • Hoffman, Alice • The drowning season • I. Title • PZ4.H6969Dr 1979 [PS3558.03447] 813'.5'4 • 78-21252 • ISBN: 0-525-09577-2 • Published simultaneously in Canada by Clarke, Irwin & Company Limited, Toronto and Vancouver • Designed by The Etheredges • 10 9 8 7 6 5 4 3 2 1 • First Edition*

For Lillie

I. TWO ESTHERS

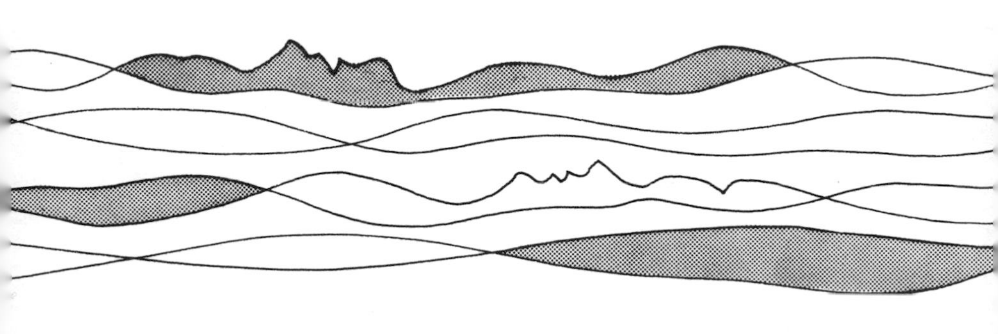

1

Once, when Esther the Black was eighteen, she sat on the porch of her grandmother's house and dragged her feet in the dust until her toes were coated and dark. She had lived within the walls that surrounded the Compound of houses owned by her grandparents all of her life, but she promised herself that this year would be different. Esther struck the head of a blue-tipped kitchen match along the railing; she lit a cigarette and tilted her denim cap back on her dark hair. Although she was the same age her grandmother was when the old woman gave birth to her first and only child, Phillip, Esther the Black looked young, she looked like any orphan scowling in the sun. The cap protected Esther's eyes, but the light was still white hot across her skin; it was the time of year they called Drowning Season, and the day would soon be too hot to sit outdoors; already the heat rose from the grass and the dust in maniac waves.

From where she sat, Esther the Black could see the harbor, and beyond that, the Sound. In the center of the group of houses was a large circular green, surrounded by feathery mimosa trees. And farther up on the porch, in a white wicker rocking chair, the girl's grandmother, Esther the White, dreamed in the sun, her long hair caught up with tiny silver pins.

Esther the Black refused to look at her grandmother; so she stared, instead, at the collection she had begun as a child which decorated her grandparents' porch and every other porch in the Compound. Sea urchin shells, green crabs, and blood sea stars rested in rows on the wooden railings, and Esther ran her foot through the dusty shadows of their skeletons. It was the first summer the girl had thought she would be free; she had finished school, she had planned to travel far from the Compound. But now, as the air closed in and the orange lilies grew so close they seemed to root between her toes, it might have been any summer of her life.

"If you sit on this porch any longer," Esther the White called to her granddaughter, "your muscles will freeze, your bones will be paralyzed, and you'll never be able to move again. That's what laziness does."

Esther the Black ignored her grandmother; she watched the lawn, where her father, Phillip, sat in a low wooden chair. Beyond the sea wall, the harbor was motionless.

"Of course you think I know nothing," Esther the White continued, as she rocked in her white wicker chair. "Of course you would rather contract the plague than listen to me."

Esther the Black scowled. All of the family was marked with a dislike for Esther the White, and that was how the girl had gotten her name. Phillip had named his daughter on a hot August day, with an ancient hostility and a smile. For although Esther the White and Mischa had severed any connection to Judaism, and had even changed their family name while living in France, Phillip was aware that children should only be named after the dead, never the living. He had had a slight interest in their ignored religion for a time, he had even tried to teach himself Hebrew, until his then current analyst had convinced him the act was regressive. Still, he knew enough to watch very carefully during the announcement of his newborn daughter's name, and he was sure he could see his mother's body suddenly tighten.

"I have to admit that I am ignoring you," Esther the Black told her grandmother. And what was the difference; she had ignored her for years. When Esther the Black's own mother Rose was too ill with hangovers, or the vapors, or sadness, Esther the White had taken charge of the girl's upbringing. And so, Esther the Black's childhood had been strict—though she rebelled. She had traded starched white blouses for schoolmates' T-shirts, she had ripped every ruffled dress, had even spilled soup on the silk scarves Esther the White tied around her neck; and when Esther the White ordered that the girl be driven to school in her grandfather's blood-colored Cadillac, Esther the Black still waited for the school bus, and she sneaked aboard like a pirate with a book bag.

"Naturally you're ignoring me." Esther the White nodded in the sun. "Otherwise you wouldn't be young and stupid."

For as long as she could remember, Esther the Black had disliked everything about her grandmother. The way she spoke, her slow, straight posture; even the way her long, pale hand reached for a silver salt shaker at the dinner table.

"If I were you," Esther the White continued, "I'd be on the beach, getting some exercise, feeling the cool water on my ankles."

The girl wanted to see her grandmother, who dressed in

linen and silk, even on the hottest days, climbing over the sea wall, now that the gate was locked for Drowning Season.

"When I was a girl, I was foolish, although not as stupid as you," Esther the White said.

Esther the Black tried to imagine her grandmother as a foolish girl, but she could not; she could only imagine what she had always known: strict orders through pale, wrinkled lips. Over the years Esther the Black's feeling had grown; it had blossomed from distaste to resentment; and finally, like a clear white flower, motionless in the heat, Esther the Black felt herself hating the woman who rocked so slowly behind her that the rocking chair scraped like claws on the wooden porch boards.

"You were never foolish," Esther the Black said.

"No." Esther the White shrugged. "I guess not," she said.

And, although Esther the White was never foolish, she had a talent for making others feel that way. Esther the Black could not help but remember the day when she was only eleven and had slipped onto the school bus for the last time. When the bus passed in front of the high iron Compound gate, she had gone to the center of the bus, sitting among local children she knew from class and recess, but whom she never talked to outside of school and whom she certainly never invited home.

"Look who's on the bus," an older girl said. "The nigger."

"I don't know what she's talking about," Esther the Black confessed to the kindergartner who shared her seat.

"Yes you do," the girl continued. "I heard your grandmother call you Esther the Black last weekend in St. Fredrics. I know that they lock you in a closet at home, so that nobody will know about you."

Esther the Black had no idea what a nigger might be, but some of the other children were now staring at her, and the kindergartner at her side was about to cry, tears welled up in his eyes.

"I'm Hawaiian," Esther the Black said quickly.

"Hah," the older girl said. "Let's hear you speak Hawaiian, big shot."

Esther the Black kept her mouth shut. For some time she had felt there was something different about her, something wrong. Her grandmother always lowered her voice when she called the girl by name, and it was always Esther the Black, never just Esther. And then, in the school bus, watched carefully by the other students, Esther wondered if Black meant something more than the color of her hair, she wondered if it might be better to have hair like her grandmother's, hair long as white chiffon.

But, before anyone could call her more names, before Esther could cry, the school bus was cut off at the corner of Main Street. The Cadillac, driven by the hired man, Cohen, had swerved in front of the bus, and Esther the Black's grandmother was pounding on the glass doors with rings on all of her fingers. The bus driver had no choice; who wouldn't open a door for Esther the White when she tossed a blue silk scarf over her shoulder and stared so coldly. And when she walked down the aisle, with posture as straight as wire, Esther the White washed silence over every grade-school child.

"Let's go," she said to Esther the Black. "The car is waiting."

Esther the Black looked out the window; she pretended not to know this woman; next to her the kindergartner had begun to sniffle.

"Did you hear me?" Esther the White said. "When I was a child I would have given anything to be driven to school in a beautiful car, rather than this." She sniffed as she looked around the bus; chewing gum stuck to the soles of her Italian shoes, peanut butter was in the air.

Esther the Black's tormentor, a fifth-grader, who wore blue plastic rimmed eyeglasses, pulled on Esther the White's silk sleeve. Esther the White turned as if she smelled something horrible, something bad.

"Is she Hawaiian?" the girl asked, pointing a finger at Esther the Black.

"It's rude to point," Esther the White told the tormentor.

"Is she?" the fifth-grader asked.

Esther the Black looked up at her grandmother. Not one muscle in the girl's face moved, not a ruffle on her blouse. Esther the White did not even look at her granddaughter, whose skin was so summer dark, whose eyes were so huge that she might have been any race, a child of anyone.

"No," Esther the White said, turning to walk out of the school bus, and signaling Esther the Black to follow. "She is not Hawaiian, but she certainly is a fool."

So, Esther the Black, the liar, the non-Hawaiian, followed her grandmother off the school bus. She did not even turn when someone poked her in the ribs. That day she would have done anything to have her grandmother as an ally, to have her story backed up, to have a smile. But Esther the Black had none of those things as she followed her grandmother off the bus; and once they were inside the Cadillac, and Cohen was speeding toward the elementary school in St. Fredrics, Esther the White lit a filter-tipped cigarette and said, "They're only envious because you ride to school in such a beautiful car. I hope you know that."

But Esther the Black knew nothing of the sort. They weren't envious; they hated her because she was embarrassed to visit them, to have Cohen waiting for her outside a tract house, leaning on the clean Cadillac and looking at his nails. They hated her because she wasn't even Hawaiian as an excuse. But Esther the Black agreed, she nodded her head yes, because her grandmother was staring at her with large, pale eyes, because her mother, Rose, had made her swear not to anger the old woman because the family depended on her, on her houses, and her wealth.

And when they pulled up to the schoolhouse, miles ahead of the bus, Esther the White handed her granddaughter a tortoise-shell comb. "You should be more embarrassed over your hair than this car," she said. "Your hair is unmanageable, like a wild dog's."

Esther the Black ran the comb through her short hair, but her hands were shaking; and try as she might, she could never weave her hair into long, fine chiffon.

As Esther the Black scowled, and imagined one of her few childhood memories, Esther the White pointed at her with a long, accusing finger.

"I had to work too hard," Esther the White was saying. "I didn't have time to be foolish."

Esther the Black wondered what sort of work her grandmother might have ever done; her hands were as smooth as ice, even now, she only cooked dinner once a week, and she never cleaned up afterward. Her only activity which might be considered work was to drive into Manhattan once a month and consult the family's accountant, Solomon Rath, and that was at an air-conditioned office on Madison Avenue, where Rath's secretary served the old woman black Russian tea and cakes.

Esther the Black had begun to think quite a lot about work since her graduation from high school. If she wanted escape she would have to find a job, and yet she was qualified to do nothing but sit in the back seat of the rusty Cadillac and tell Cohen which way to turn. If she was not careful, if she was not quick, she would find herself married to the accountant's son, Ira Rath. Esther stubbed out her cigarette in the dust. Ira Rath was now at college in Vermont, but he had been expected to become Esther's husband since their first introduction. The family had chosen him for her in the summer when she was twelve.

"It will please your grandmother," Rose had told Esther. "And that's important. His family is good, and we'll need an accountant in our family when the old woman dies. Phillip doesn't know the difference between a stock and a bond."

So, that summer, before Esther the Black even knew what

marriage was, there was a dinner party to introduce the two. Silk scarves moved like snakes, like air, as Rose offered canapés of sour cream and chicken to the elder Raths. "What do you think of him?" she whispered to Esther the Black.

Esther the Black swept three canapés from the plate. "I hate him," she said.

"Please," Rose had said, peering across the room at her mother-in-law, Esther the White. "Our future depends on this liaison. Do you want to be disowned? Do you want your father to lose control of his inheritance and be sent to Rockland or Pilgrim State?"

Esther the Black just swung her legs beneath a scratchy crinoline, and was silent as her grandfather Mischa and Solomon Rath discussed the children's engagement. Across the canapés, Ira, who was not yet fourteen, winked.

There was no doubt now, six years later, Esther the Black had not been trained to be anything but a wife. She needed a job and a means of escape, and she winced when Esther the White called from her rocking chair, "Someday you may learn to take my advice."

Esther the Black shaded her eyes and stared upward; a helicopter, which flew in tourists from New York City to St. Fredrics, circled above the Compound. Esther the Black's father, Phillip, rose from his lawn chair and waved a hand at the sky.

"Look at him," Esther the Black smiled as her father greeted the helicopter, and she watched him as she would some darling child.

"Just look at him?" Esther the White said. "We have to do more than that. We have to watch him."

When the helicopter had flown by them, Esther the Black stood on the porch stairs, and she strained to see the green stone beach which had been littered with scales, with fish heads, with fins. The poachers, a local band of fishermen who had sold Mischa the land for the Compound twenty years before when he had first planned to build the most luxurious housing development in the state, had been into the run of bluefish. The fishermen had never left the harbor, even though Mischa had hired Cohen to guard the beach. Now, Esther the Black watched from the porch as Cohen walked slowly along the stones; he sat on the last remaining dock, one the family still used occasionally, and he stared at the traces left behind by the poachers. He moved his foot in a watery circle; his foot disappeared into the water, then a leg—finally, Esther the Black could no longer see him; he had disappeared into the harbor.

And as he disappeared, Esther the Black's great aunt, Lisa, walked across the green from her large cottage and leaned on the porch railing. "That's right," she said to no one in particular in a thick Viennese accent Esther the White despised. "You go swimming, Cohen, and then you tell everyone you are a gardener who is planting seaweed. If my sweetest husband could see this, Cohen would be fired in a minute."

Esther the White raised her eyebrows. It was her husband, Mischa, and not Lisa's, who paid Cohen's salary. "When exactly was the last time you paid for anything?" she asked her sister-in-law.

Lisa hissed, but then was silent; true, she had been a nonpaying guest at the Compound for years, but she was the wife of Mischa's brother. And a brother who had suffered plenty. "I'm just making a comment," she told Esther the White.

Esther the Black ignored both women; she strained to see Cohen; his arms were breaking through the calm water. And although he was a strong swimmer—and had taught Esther the Black the backstroke and the butterfly—he was getting to be an old man, and it was summer; now even the fishermen called summer the Drowning Season. They swore that Mischa and his family had brought Drowning Season with them to the Compound, and now even the most experienced swimmer, the oldest fisherman, was in danger of drowning on the calmest days.

Not that the superstition stopped their poaching. They still rowed boats far into the Sound, they still carried nets, and transistor radios, and knives; a curse was a curse, but they had to live.

And so, at night, in Drowning Season, the family could listen from their beds, they could hear the splashing of gills and arms. In the morning, before sunrise, when the sounds of struggling fish were replaced by the loud music from the transistor radios the fishermen listened to, men and women called from one painted boat to another, and they brought their woven circle of nets closer and closer to a center.

All of the women on the porch watched Cohen; not one of them would have been surprised if he had suddenly sunk to the bottom like a stone. The temperature climbed higher and higher into the nineties, the air was thick, the frogs began to call.

"Shit," Lisa said, and she tossed her red-and-blond streaked hair as she heard the chorus. "They are in need of being cooked up," she said of the frogs who had gathered at the sea wall for more than twenty years, as if the wall of sandstone had taken some frogs who wandered inland by surprise. Those frogs were trapped; for years they had been separated from the water, they had forgotten how to swim, they were landlocked now that the hinges on the sea-wall gate were so old they had rusted, now that the wood of the gate was scarred with barnacles. And because they could neither fly nor climb stone, the frogs sang, at odd hours of the day, alone or in a chorus.

"What I would like to do is cook them up with butter," Lisa said. "In the biggest pot." She examined the large diamond ring on her finger. "Ach, the headaches that gives me," she said of the frogs' song.

"Don't say that," Esther the Black said, because Lisa cooked all of the family's meals, except on Friday night, when Esther the White honored them with her cooking. "How could anyone eat frogs?" the girl said.

Lisa, who still considered herself to be Viennese, although Max had brought her to America years before, wrinkled up her nose and sniffed. "Shows how much you know, miss," she said. "It's a delicacy. Anyone in Europe would know it for a fact. In Europe they know what to do with frogs who scream."

Esther the White touched a white linen handkerchief to her forehead; she did not want to hear her sister-in-law's thick voice when the day was so hot, and the shells of false angel's wings littered the green stone beach, and the pain in her side which had begun last winter was strung tightly, a sharp wire somewhere beneath her skin. "Stop that," she told Lisa. "I'm not interested in your recipes for water frogs."

"Oh, well," Lisa glared. "Pardon me."

"What nonsense," Esther the White murmured.

"I do beg your pardon," Lisa hissed.

"Talk, talk," Esther the White said, wishing that she had gotten a larger prescription of codeine during her last doctor's visit. "That's all either of you can do."

Esther the Black turned, and when she thought the old woman had looked away she narrowed her eyes at her grandmother.

"I saw that," Esther the White said. "Don't think I didn't see the face you made. Don't think you're so smart."

"Such a lovely family," Lisa sighed. "But you'll excuse me if I don't stay for the arguing. Because today I'm making pies, and your arguing I need like a hole in the head, like a flea on the skin." She walked around to the kitchen door.

"You too," Esther the White said, hoping that she would be able to walk up the stairs to her own room, thinking of what lie she might tell if someone found her doubled over in pain on the stairway landing. "Go," she told her granddaughter. "Get out of here. I have no time for you and your dirty looks, or your smugness."

Esther the Black edged off the porch steps. Her face grew hot, her veins moved like seas. "Who do you think you're talking to?" she said to her grandmother.

"You," Esther the White said. "You, Esther the Black. Go away."

Esther the Black tilted her cap over her eyes. "I was just going," she said, more determined than ever to find a job and escape. "I don't need you."

"Good," Esther the White shrugged as she watched Esther the Black drag her feet through the dust.

Esther the Black's shoulders were still shaking with anger when she reached the circular green; the lawn beneath her feet was thick, well kept by Cohen, who was not only the Compound guard, but its landscape artist as well. She carried a pair of leather sandals in one hand, and she smiled when she saw her father, even though her view of him was ghostly across the stream of moving, mounting heat. The smell of honeysuckle had gotten stuck, it hung in the air. Phillip rested his head against the back of his lawn chair, his eyes gazed calmly upward. He was in his early forties, and the beard which grew in haphazard patches on his jaw was already gray.

"Going?" Phillip said to Esther the Black as she neared him.

"Only to St. Fredrics," Esther the Black answered, thinking that she could not stand one more summer of silent heat, of orders and advice from Esther the White. Esther the Black had decided to search the shops for a job; like everyone else in the Compound, except for Mischa and Esther the White, she had no money of her own, only a weekly allowance. Her own money would mean a chance to escape from this place where the honeysuckle had simply taken over, even though Phillip had ordered Cohen to plant nothing but white flowers. Gardenias were fed nails, and still they withered. Lilies grew like wax, odorless and still. Bridal wreath, begonias, small white roses with yellow centers all grew like ice. The Compound was simply not the right climate.

"Damned heat," Phillip said lazily, although he sat in the shade of a birchwood tree. His hands rested in his lap like white gloves. "What do you say," Phillip smiled, "that we go for a walk later on today?" He winked at his daughter like a loser at the track.

Esther the Black told him no; she was afraid to break the rules of Drowning Season, and the family had long ago declared that walks were off limits for Phillip. For him a walk only meant a scramble over the sea wall, over the green stones, which could so easily cut bare feet. A walk into the water, water which moved so slowly that it seemed to have no tide. A sea desert, a harbor thick with mirages.

Phillip nodded at his daughter's answer. His eyes were closing. "Damned heat," he said again of the season which belonged to him, which had been named for whatever it was that drew him to the water. Closer and closer; any harbor or stream would do. This need, or habit, or odd desire had begun in the summer of his sixteenth year. The family, Phillip and his parents, had lived in London, moving from house to house, although Esther the White was itching to get to New York. They lived in a house or a flat for only as long as it took Mischa to strip the wallpaper, to stain and wax the floors, install new plumbing, and sell at a profit.

The first time Phillip's desire struck, the wallpaper applied in the new flat was large pink flowers splashed onto cream-colored silk. The water he walked into was the Serpentine. The lake reached his knees, his waist, his chest. Before long the water had risen to his neck.

A rower in a rented boat called out and pushed an oar toward Phillip. Two policemen ruined their summer uniforms. A duck's wing was stepped on and crushed by a panicked onlooker who wore a black linen suit. When he was bodily returned to the renovated Notting Hill flat, Phillip gave no explanations for his act.

Esther the White had shrugged. "He wanted to drown," she said.

"He didn't know what he was doing," Mischa insisted, as he angrily threw a peppermint into his mouth and stared at his son. "Look at him," Mischa demanded. "Does he know what he's doing?"

Phillip was dripping lake water onto the highly polished floor. One pants leg was rolled up to his knee. He smiled slightly.

Esther the White looked him up and down. "He wanted to drown," she repeated.

Later, they discovered that Esther the White had been right from the start. There was a new attempt every summer, and once Esther's beloved passage money, which was to take the family to New York, was spent so that Phillip could spend the summer at a private clinic, where he managed to keep his head in the sink long enough to pass out. By the time Phillip was twenty, no one called July and August summer: the season had found another title.

It was habit for every member of the family to daily persuade Phillip not to leave the Compound in July and August, the hot months when the water called. On mornings when Phillip sighed and tremors ran through his pale hands, he was locked in the smallest pink cottage, reserved for Drowning Season, this year and forever. A padlock was placed on the door, and Phillip was served jasmine tea with honey, Valium, Thorazine, and cinnamon toast.

And now there was that rumor, begun by the fishermen, that a watery curse surrounded the harbor. Strangers whispered about her father when Esther the Black walked through town, and Phillip's medical history was legend at the local hospital. Occasionally tourists who had rented fishing boats in St. Fredrics, and who had heard of Drowning Season, moored at the very edge of the harbor; but through their binoculars all they could see was the fading group of pink houses, the thick lawn, and the deserted beach. No one had drowned in the harbor for more than five years, when a young fisherman was washed up onto the green stones during an unseasonable storm. But the fishermen continued to whisper, in their wooden squatters' shacks and in dark doorways in St. Fredrics, that the harbor would continue to drown innocent men and women until it found the one it searched for. And they refused to call Phillip by his name—instead they referred to him as the Drowned Man. Yet, many fishermen had been lost in the harbor, in storms or summer gales, and Phillip, the Drowned Man, continued to sleep in the sun. He slept each summer through, dressed in a thin blue bathrobe, his mouth dry from the tranquilizers he swallowed each morning, his eyes staring at the sky.

Now, he spoke absently. "I'm waiting," he said to Esther the Black.

"I'll be back soon," Esther reassured him, but Phillip had already turned from her. He didn't listen, didn't care, for he hadn't tricked her into helping him walk away from the Compound.

Esther the Black cut across the Compound lawn, and as she did she imagined walking along the harbor beach with Phillip. If she had been free to take him there, he would have seen hermit crabs, clear jellyfish, the shells of mussels coated with barnacles which grew in the shape of roses. His eyes would be closed, his feet would pass over the rocky green stones without a scratch. But, Esther was not free to show him any of these things. For years, Mischa had threatened to send Phillip upstate, to cut off Phillip's stream of analysts and clinics. The old man claimed that there was not the money there had once been; Rath, the accountant, had made some bad investments in a chemical plant in New Jersey, and land taxes were higher than ever, they were killing him. And although

Esther the White was still driven to Manhattan regularly to check the books, the last dollars were being drained, cognac was no longer ordered for Lisa and Max in crates, and Mischa had put off buying a new car for so long that the Cadillac was an antique coated with rust.

As Esther the Black walked across the Compound, Dr. Otto, Phillip's newest analyst, who vacationed in St. Fredrics each summer, drove past in his yellow MG. Esther the Black turned to wave as he sped by her, and it was then that she noticed Esther the White on the porch. She was still watching. She moved in her rocking chair, waiting like a hawk for Esther the Black to be foolish. They stared at each other, but there was no recognition on Esther the White's face. She sat like a piece of white glass in the sun.

Even though Esther the Black would have never believed it, her grandmother was then thinking of her as she rocked back and forth in the white wicker chair. There was no doubt about it, it had been Esther the White who had raised the girl. Both of Esther the Black's parents were incompetent, they had had a child in hopes of pleasing Esther the White, but once Esther the Black was born Rose could not be moved from her TV and gin, and Phillip was busy marking off the days on the calendar till Drowning Season. So, when she was past forty, Esther the White had been handed a child whose very name was an insult; and she had done the best she could, considering she had never liked children, not even her own.

As she watched her granddaughter leave the Compound, Esther the White believed that she had failed. All of the girl's training seemed wasted. Again and again, Esther the White had stressed the importance of appearance for a woman who wanted a life of ease, a life without fear; and yet there the girl was, one hand on her hip, barefoot, peering out from beneath a boy's cap, like a vagabond or a beggar. When Esther the Black was very young, her rebellions were small; and when she was particularly lonely she begged to sit near Esther the White's dressing table and she would watch with interest as Esther the White knotted a silk scarf in an intricate bow. But now, the two barely spoke; and every time Esther the White felt the brief desire to be close, she could see the girl's shoulders stiffen, and before she knew it she was reprimanding her posture, and then it was too late. Then, the girl would not listen to anything she had to say, and Esther the White was not certain what would happen if she had had the chance to speak; anything might have risen up—feathers, or words, or tears. Anything at all.

For some time Esther the White had continued to watch her granddaughter, waiting for a moment which did not come. She put off reaching out to Esther the Black just as she had put off her doctor's appointment, until the appointment had drifted by with months and forgetfulness, and fear. Esther the White knew that she had to hurry; either that, or fail; and there would be no reconciliation. But where to begin? When the old woman, from the chair where she sat shielded in sunglasses and scarves like a lizard on the rocks, warned the girl against growing too dark in the sun, Esther the Black would sit on the beach until her skin turned the shade of dark, wet earth, until her eyes were ripe. As far as Esther the Black was concerned, there was nothing to talk about; she walked through the iron Compound gates, and as her grandmother's pale stare chilled her through the waves of heat, Esther decided that she would take any damn job she could find.

She began to walk down Route 16; a mile or so south of the Compound the road would lead her to St. Fredrics. She slipped on her leather sandals, and listened to the soles scraping through the brown needles of grass along the side of the road. There was little traffic; once a car horn honked at her, and the sound echoed for a long time, like the call of an owl. Each side of the road was bordered by wild orange lilies whose centers were heart-shaped and purple. Esther the Black kept her eyes down; she barely noticed when the town began. She walked past the drive-in movie theater she had never gone to, past the Shell gas station and the McDonald's where Cohen had once taken her.

She could no longer bear to live in the Compound, she could no longer behave. Esther the Black soon reached the St. Fredrics docks, where ferries and fishing boats moved on their tethers even when the water seemed absent of motion. Here, alongside a café which boasted the world's greatest clam chowder, Esther the Black bought a copy of the St. Fredrics *Herald* at a newspaper kiosk. She walked on to the center of town, sat on a green bench, and unfolded the paper. Behave, Esther the Black thought, as if she were a poor relation, or a bear that danced.

She had no intention of marrying Ira Rath; she never had. But what could she do instead? If Esther had paid more attention to her grandmother she would have known how to set a table or serve sangría or wear silk pajamas: tricks to catch a husband other than Ira. But she did not even know how to do this. Esther's uncle Max spoke of managing a circus in Europe, and Esther the White balanced the books, but Cohen was the only one who seemed to work, and from him Esther the Black had learned a great deal about gardenias and strawberries, fertilizer and mulch. But she doubted that anyone would hire her as a landscape artist, she was not a man and she had no references.

Esther sighed and shredded the classified section; buses came and went, but she stayed on the green bench. Across the street were a coffee house, a bait shop, and a shell store which fooled tourists into buying Pacific conch shells as native to the St. Fredrics harbor. There was also a fish store, with a window display of plastic sea anemones and a plaster model of a blue shark suspended by string so that it seemed to fly somewhere behind the glass. Around the doorway, some of the Compound poachers had gathered. They stood wearing their familiar mark—a blue headband wrapped around their foreheads. Esther looked up from her torn newspaper and watched as the fish-store owner, who had just bought a crate of mussels and bluefish, suggested that the poachers keep away from the slick sawdust-coated doorway. They frightened away the shoppers; suburban women from the new housing developments which tightly encircled the old port town were not likely to push by a group of lingering, thoroughly fishy men. "Out of here, my friends," the fish-store owner said. "Out of here, bums," he joked.

Esther knew the fishermen well, though they never greeted each other in public places, and her grandmother would have been shocked to know how many evenings Esther the Black had spent in their campground when Cohen, serving as Esther's babysitter, and later her friend, drank bourbon and played cards and Esther the Black learned how to kiss and how to scale fish. It would have been easy to work for the fishermen; she was as strong as any of the women who rowed out into the harbor when darkness fell, and it would have not taken her long to learn how to repair a net. But they would never had had her; she had grown up in their encampment, but she was still the Drowned Man's daughter, and many of the old men were convinced that she carried the harbor's curse with her.

And even if they had offered her a job, digging the mud for mussels or clams, cleaning fishhooks, or rowing her own small boat, they could never afford to pay her anything but her weight in fish. They were poor, they lived in shacks and trailers, and many of the young men and women had left to find their fortune in Florida or California. Esther the Black watched as the fishermen walked down Main Street, and when one of the young men stopped to slip on a pair of yellow sunglasses and offer himself as a guide to a couple who carried a picnic hamper, Esther the Black sat up so straight, even her grandmother would have been proud of her posture.

In the window of the old Woolworth's, just behind the fisherman's left ear, was a help-wanted sign. Esther left her newspaper and her cap on the bench; she raced across the street, not waiting for the streetlight to turn, dodging between the moving cars. She rushed down the aisles of the store pleading to see the manager as the slow wooden fans droned overhead. Esther the Black bit her fingers, she shifted her weight from foot to foot. The store manager drummed his nails on a glass counter top and eyed Esther's enthusiasm coldly; but she was used to cold glances and she said, "I can do it. I can sell anything. Give me a break."

"A break?" the manager said. "This isn't Hollywood. It's only part time in cosmetics."

But all the same, by the time Esther got through with him, the manager felt like a producer, a director, a giver of breaks.

"All right," he told her, as her nervous fingers fluttered and the lies she was inventing about experience and previous employment flew like birds, faster and faster, leaving the taste of feathers in her mouth. "Don't tell me again about your sick relatives. Don't tell me how terrific you are. Prove it."

And by the time Esther had been fitted for a pink uniform, and given the lowdown on the previous cosmetics salesgirl, a woman named Ronelle, who had been caught with forty cartons of Maybelline eyeliner in the trunk of her Mustang, the day had grown late. And Esther the Black, who was thinking about possibilities, about not behaving, walked back to the Compound without looking at the road. Instead, she merely followed the scent of the orange flowers which grew by the side of the road, until she was home.

2

In the morning, when her granddaughter was reporting for her first day at work, Esther the White was awakened from her light sleep by a pain as sharp as an alarm. Whatever her illness was, Esther the White could no longer ignore it. She had always been an insomniac, but now she could not sleep at all, and except for a few soft hours in the earliest morning, sleeplessness had become as common as night. Often, she spent hours staring into the dark and remembering her past; and the memories and insomnia intertwined and confused her, even in the daylight hours, so that she never knew past from present; sometimes, as she walked over the Compound lawn, Esther did not know if her heel would fall into harbor sand or into the frozen winter earth of her childhood.

The pain which had forced her to the doctor's office last winter was cold and metallic; it made Esther dig her fingernails into her own palms, until bloodlines formed. She had run out of codeine, she had run out of time, she could put it off no longer. She summoned Cohen.

"Of course," she told Cohen, when he met her at the foot of the porch steps, "you're not to tell anyone where you've driven me."

Cohen could never say no to Esther the White; he would not have even tried. He was insulted that she did not trust him to keep his mouth shut, after the secrets they had shared. "What am I?" he said, as he opened the back door of the car, and Esther the White gathered her linen coat, and slipped into the back seat. "A spy, maybe? A member of the CIA?"

"Dear man," Esther the White said, and Cohen cringed at her tone, "I thought it was a perfectly reasonable request. A well-phrased request."

"The phrasing was perfect," Cohen agreed. "Very nice. I couldn't fault it."

"Thank you," Esther the White said, and she stared out the window as Cohen drove down the Compound road. When he stopped at the iron gate, Esther leaned forward and tapped his shoulder. "Go ahead," she said. "Drive."

Cohen turned to face the back seat. "Certainly," he said. "I'd like to. But tell me, Mrs., where am I driving to?"

Esther the White gave Cohen the address of the doctor's office on one of the high, sloping residential streets of St. Fredrics. And although the day was warm, and jays flew in circles around the Cadillac's antenna, Esther the White felt chilled, even in her linen coat, and she asked Cohen to keep his window rolled up.

"You want the heater on, too?" Cohen shrugged.

A cigarette was constantly caught between Cohen's lips,

and ash fell down the front of his short-sleeved shirt as he talked; he always wore a black beret as his driving cap. Esther the White laughed at herself, and conceded; just because she was cold did not mean everyone else was, too; Cohen could open his window. But, she kept hers closed; she preferred to look at the landscape through the closed glass. As they drove down Route 16, Esther pinned up stray strands of hair which had fallen from her chignon. When they stopped at a light, Esther caught a glimpse of herself in the rear-view mirror. Her hair had somehow turned from platinum to white, wrinkles had jumped like lizards onto her face, her eyes were nearly colorless.

"Cohen," she sighed. "I'm old."

Cohen swallowed; he was afraid to look, he was afraid that she was right; but, when he raised his eyes and saw her face in the mirror, she was young, as young as she had ever been. The light turned green, but Cohen forgot to step on the gas.

"You'd better drive," Esther the White suggested, when the cars behind them began to honk their horns.

Cohen steered toward the high, green streets of the oldest section of town. They drove in silence, each thinking about their own separate arrivals in New York, until Esther tapped her fingernails on the leather upholstery and said, "This is it."

Cohen pulled over to the curb in front of a large yellow Victorian which had once belonged to a sea captain who had died, quite slowly, in the attic early in the century. Now, a separate entrance led to an office, and the doctor's name and business hours swung from chains on a wooden post.

Cohen was busy staring at himself in the rear-view mirror; he wondered if Esther the White thought he also was growing old. He hadn't given himself time to shave, he had planned to spend the day in the fishermen's campground, playing cards and drinking bourbon, until Esther summoned him. And now the stubble of hair which grew on his chin was gray. In the rear-view mirror Cohen could see that Esther's eyes were closed, and her pale hand stroked her throat, as if something strange had been caught inside, under her tongue. Cohen looked at her, and then at the sign on the doctor's office. He was an idiot; Esther was ill, and he should have seen it before. He might have, but every time he looked at her he saw a younger Esther, the one who stood in the kitchen fixing lemonade the first time he spoke to her.

He panicked, he forgot himself, he called her by name for the first time in twenty years. "Esther?" he said.

The way he said her name, the mere saying of her name after all the years, when they barely spoke, when he was careful not to look at her, not even when she poured him a glass of wine at the Friday-night meal, pulled at Esther. She raised her eyes; in the mirror, floating above his face, above his clear gray eyes, was the face of a younger man. He hadn't aged a bit, he was the same man he had been years ago.

"Don't look at me," Esther the White said. "Don't look at me that way, there is nothing wrong." She had said almost the same exact words when Cohen had waited at the curb of an apartment building in Forest Hills, while Esther the White took the elevator up to the abortionist who would get rid of whatever Mischa had planted inside of her. But that had been years before, and Esther the White had not been afraid herself.

"If there's nothing wrong, why don't you want anyone to know where you are?" Cohen asked.

"That's the way I am." Esther shrugged. "Private. You should know that by now."

"Esther," he said her name again. "Who are you kidding? This is me, Cohen."

"And this is me," Esther said, as she reached for the door handle.

When Cohen heard the click of the door handle, when he knew she was about to walk out of the car, he stopped her. He had not taken the elevator with her up to the third-floor abortionist's office twelve years before. This time he would accompany her. "Listen," Cohen said. "Let me come with you. Who sits alone in a waiting room?"

Esther the White let go of the door handle; she sat far back in her seat, and gripped one hand with the other. This time she was frightened.

"I don't think so," she told Cohen.

"Frankly," Cohen said, "there are dozens of magazines in that doctor's office I haven't gotten around to reading yet. It would be a treat for me."

The pain was throbbing in her side, and she was already late for her appointment. She imagined walking up the brick path, leaning on Cohen's arm, with her head light as air. She reached over and opened the door. "You're a gentleman," she said. "As usual."

One of Esther's feet was already outside; her heel was balancing on the hot pavement. Cohen stuck his head out the open window. "All right," he said. "But don't forget I'm here if you change your mind. Especially if they have *Sports Illustrated.* I love that. I could read that for hours."

Esther the White smiled. "All right," she said. "I'll remember."

As he watched her walk away, Cohen rested an elbow on the steering wheel, and then he lit another cigarette. He sighed; he thought about time. He wished he had a pocket calculator; he had always wanted one. But, even without a calculator, by the time Esther the White had walked down the brick path to the old Victorian house, Cohen had figured out her age. He had known it was impossible for her to be old. In the hot Cadillac, with cigarette ash dotting the front of his white shirt, Cohen had figured that he and Esther the White were, within a year or two, the same age.

His figures began with the year 1956; it was then, three years before Esther the Black was born, and two weeks after Esther the White's fortieth birthday, that Cohen arrived at the Compound. It was winter when he took a taxi from the ferry to the iron gate, and the ground was hard, ice-coated sand, and Cohen did not know then if he had been graced with a challenge, or fated to be a landscape artist in a place where nothing would ever grow.

It was Esther the White who kept Cohen at the Compound, long after he discovered that the earth was far too sandy for a landscape artist to have any duty other than a continuous replanting of what was already dead. He had been a wanderer since the day he had fled Russia, he had traveled to Europe and South America and Florida; but when he fell in love with Esther the White he became rooted in the Compound for the rest of his life. After that he no longer protested that he served not only as a gardener, but a guard as well, keeping the poachers away from the Compound beach. After falling in love he did not complain that his residence was the lighthouse. And anyway, he had had night jobs and day jobs on three continents as a short-order cook, a salesman, a clock repairman, and a tailor; so he had no preference for day or night, and he ignored the light which blinked constantly, whether he was asleep or dreaming, or studying the horticulture books that would teach him the skills he had already promised Mischa he had. And even now, years later, as he raked the beach of debris, or worked on the yard in the sunlight, he suffered from hallucinations which were black and white spots dancing before his open eyes.

He had practically raised Esther the Black; and he had studied so well that he was able to teach her the name of every plant that grew in the Compound. It was Cohen, and no one else, who caused Esther the Black to sob when he told her that every jellyfish on the shore was there because it was dead, and not resting in the sunshine the way swimmers did. It was Cohen who explained to her why her father could not walk along the beach in summertime; why Phillip often could not even leave his cottage. And now, all Esther the Black talked about was escape. And each time Cohen would laugh and say,

"Escape from the Compound? Do you think there's something better somewhere else?" although he, himself, had thought seriously of heading back to Manhattan that first week in 1956, before he spoke with Esther the White.

He knew nothing about gardens, and he was not used to the loneliness of the Compound; when he was alone in the city at least there were other bodies, in Laundromats and coffee shops, touching against him, accidentally or on purpose. Here, the crickets and the frogs made him crazy. And he thought he would go crazier still, with no woman, no liquor store, not even a card game, not even a dog. He thought he would go mad, until he met the fishermen, and Esther the White.

"Boss, I think maybe I'm going nuts out here in the country," Cohen told Mischa after only a few days.

"Don't call me boss," Mischa had said. In fact, it had been Esther the White who had chosen Cohen's letter from among the other job applicants. "Cohen?" Mischa had said. "A Jew with no references? That's not your style."

And Esther the White, who had forced Mischa to Anglicize their last name, and give up every prayer, every inch of Judaism, shrugged her shoulders. "He'll be more honest than the others," she said.

"You don't believe that," Mischa said.

"No," Esther the White had admitted. But the man was Russian, he might have come from a town close to their own, a town she despised, had nightmares about, a town she was drawn to in her imagining, and could not forget. "Hire him," she had said.

And so, Mischa never considered himself Cohen's boss. "Do your job, take care of the gardens, go out in the rowboat and get rid of the poachers," Mischa had told him. "You don't have time to go crazy if you're working for me."

Cohen shrugged; and he rowed out into the harbor. For four nights he watched, as the poachers worked around him. Nets fell into the water; men and women called to each other, and, as the sun rose, all of the boats disappeared from the harbor, except Cohen's own painted rowboat. On the fifth night Cohen decided he was not only a failure as a gardener and a guard, but as a human being as well. He fell asleep in his boat. When he awoke he heard the movement of another boat's oars, the raspy breathing of another man's throat. Cohen tried to light a cigarette, but the match was wet and the flame sputtered and died in his hands, between his fingers. There was no light but half a moon, and Cohen could not see the fisherman's face, he could see only the reflection of a face which moved in the waves. Cohen briefly closed his eyes; he hoped that he would not drop an oar into the depths of the harbor, he hoped that he would not forget what his job was.

"What will you catch," the fisherman said to Cohen, "with no line and no bait?"

"What we've got," Cohen said across the darkness, "is a situation that's uncomfortable. Wouldn't you say that was true?"

"No trouble," the other said. "No sweat."

"Ah, maybe not for you, but for me . . ." Cohen touched his heart. "It's my duty to be the guard of this harbor."

"What sort of job is that?" the other shrugged.

"A job for an idiot," Cohen agreed. "But a man who's close to forty isn't getting younger, and you take the jobs you get."

Most of the boats in the harbor had begun to move toward the eastern section of the Compound, which had never been developed; Cohen could not see men and women, only blue bands of material which shone in the darkness—headbands the fishermen wore as talismans to protect them against drowning.

"Just tell them to keep the Drowned Man away from our harbor," Cohen's fisherman said, before he, too, rowed his boat toward land.

Cohen watched a circle of sun rise above the Sound; and then he rowed back to shore, tethered the boat to the Compound dock, and knocked on the door of Mischa's study to ask who the Drowned Man was.

Mischa looked up from the real-estate section of *The New York Times.* "I don't give reports to you, Cohen," he said. "When you start getting results, when those beggars are out of my harbor, then come to me. Then ask me questions."

Cohen found Lisa, who had arrived at the Compound with her husband, Max, only a few months before Cohen, on the porch of her cottage. She stared at Cohen coolly; she had never liked Russians, and she couldn't understand why Mischa hadn't hired a black, like other Americans. "So," Lisa said. "Now the Russian wants to know about the Drowned Man. Well, that is for me to know and for you to find out."

Cohen was now wary. This place is giving me the shivers, it gives me the creeps, he thought.

He thought about packing his suitcase; he thought he could not last another day. Then, more than twenty years ago, the Sound was clear water, there was no smog over the outline of Connecticut's shore, no supermarkets or housing developments had yet sprung from the heads of real-estate barons. It was, more or less, the country. And this, for a man who had known Krakow, and Rio, and Manhattan, was depressing. And more—when the crickets sang like whirlwinds, when the fisherman in the harbor whispered about a curse, and the night was without neon lights and traffic signals, the Compound was terrifying. Cohen was chain smoking; a slight twitch had developed beneath his left eye; and he gave himself twenty-four hours to find out the truth about the Drowned Man, or he would be on the morning ferry to New York City.

Cohen went to Esther the White. She had been with the rest of the family at the gate to greet Cohen when he first arrived; but a silk scarf had been wrapped around her head, her eyes were covered by dark glasses, she had stared at the earth, and Cohen had barely noticed her, he was too busy shaking hands with Mischa, and his brother, the dwarf. Now, he found her in the kitchen of the main house, and the first words he spoke to her were, "Who is the Drowned Man?"

Cohen spoke abruptly, because he was standing just inside the door, and he was afraid that the draft from the open door would disturb Esther, who was halving lemons on a wooden cutting board. She was forty then, but the long white streaks in her pale hair which hung nearly to her waist were not visible, and when she stared at Cohen with her sea-colored eyes, and absentmindedly stirred too much sugar into the pitcher of fresh lemonade, she looked like a young girl. Cohen could not remember seeing anyone like her, not even in Rio or Manhattan. No one's hand had ever been as light, like a feathered bird which somehow managed to hold a knife. No one's hair had danced with a draft so softly, not in any summer of Cohen's life.

"He's my son," Esther told Cohen. "He has a problem with suicide attempts."

"Well, then." Cohen shrugged. "Then we certainly can't get rid of him just to please the fishermen."

"Certainly not," Esther agreed, as she watched Cohen flee through the brass-hinged door.

Cohen thought of her all that day, as he drove Mischa's new Cadillac into St. Fredrics to pick up topsoil at a greenhouse; and later that night he was still thinking of her as he rowed out to meet the fisherman.

"Listen," Cohen said. "I can't help you out with the Drowned Man. The Drowned Man stays. They put him in a special cottage in the summer, so I haven't met him yet. But he's the boss's son, and I can tell you right now, they won't even consider getting rid of him."

The fisherman stared at Cohen without blinking. Then he took a package of thin, black cigars from his pocket and offered Cohen a smoke. When the poachers heard that Mischa had hired a guard, they were ready to defend themselves. The family's accountant, Solomon Rath, who had purchased the land for Mischa when the family still lived in London, had vowed that the fishermen would never be forced out of the harbor. But as soon as the architects and the builders had finished, Rath had sent out an eviction notice. This time the fishermen were ready to fight back. Some of the younger men drove to Brooklyn and bought shotguns and .45-caliber pistols, even though very few of them actually knew how to fire guns. The families that feared for their children's safety packed their clothes and their fishing gear and moved on, to the east end of the island, or to Florida, where they lived in trailer parks. But the old men in the encampment who had been threatened by town officials and local citizens for longer than they could remember said, "Wait. Let's see what happens." And the old women, when they heard that a guard had been hired, sighed and said, "Wait. We'll see that nothing will happen." And now, the fisherman smoked his cigar, and he wondered what kind of guard the family had hired; a guard who not only made reports to his boss, but to a fisherman as well; a guard who sighed and laid back in his rowboat to watch the cigar smoke circle in the clear night air.

But the fisherman did not know that Cohen had been Esther the White's choice, and that Esther the White did not give a damn if the poachers camped in the wild eastern section of the Compound, and she did not give a damn if they caught a million bluefish in the Compound's waters. As far as she was concerned, Cohen's only job was to keep Phillip alive. Others thought Cohen was a failure—and it was true, the poachers still streamed fish entrails across Mischa's seaside, the ivy Cohen planted on the sea wall withered, and roses often appeared where wisteria had been ordered, but Esther the White had been right when she had first chosen Cohen—in nearly a quarter of a century, Phillip had not killed himself. That had been Esther's goal when she first pulled Cohen's letter out of its envelope. It was true, the man had no qualifications, but Esther believed that a man who could not do any of the jobs he was hired to do would naturally gravitate to other jobs. He would feel guilty because he was inadequate, he would be indebted to the family who had hired him despite this, and he would be as faithful to Phillip as a St. Bernard.

It would not have concerned Esther the White that Cohen was slowly becoming friendly with the fishermen. Because by the time Cohen had begun to spend evenings playing cards with the poachers, he had already saved Phillip from drowning on a hot August night. Esther the White might have raised an eyebrow had she learned that by the time Esther the Black was born, and Phillip had been rescued by the landscape artist three times, Cohen had known quite a few of the women in the fishermen's camp as lovers. He had even become seriously involved with Nina, the sister of the fisherman he had spoken to during his first night as the Compound's guard. But Esther the White would have done no more than raise an eyebrow; and by the time the landscape artist had saved Phillip's life five times, there was nothing anyone could say that would have made Esther the White fire Cohen.

So, Cohen played card games regularly, and he was even taught to play Bolo, the fish game where the form of a skeleton is rebuilt. He loved to sleep with Nina, because her skin was like cool, moving water, even on the hottest night. The years moved for Cohen, with cards, and bourbon, soon with caring for Esther the Black; but although he had a lover, it wasn't Esther the White. When Nina grew tired of her life's hard work and decided to move on to Florida, where an aunt through marriage ran a soft-ice-cream concession in Pompano Beach, she offered Cohen a free train ticket and a life of soft ice cream; but Cohen declined. He had to, he didn't love her. Esther the Black was in the back seat of the Cadillac the day Cohen drove Nina to the ferry; at five years old, she was smart enough to look the other way when Nina kissed Cohen goodbye and whispered once again that she could afford train tickets for two to Fort Lauderdale. Esther the Black had grown up in the fishermen's encampment; the first time Cohen had taken her there she had been two, and he had found her alone on the porch of her parents' cottage, in the season when Phillip was locked in his special cottage, and Rose couldn't face anything but gin and tonics. From the start Esther the Black had kicked off her shoes the minute they crossed over to the eastern section of the Compound, from the start she understood when Cohen placed his finger to his lips when he deposited her on her parents' doorstep. That day, at the ferry, Cohen bought Esther a treat as they walked down the docks to see Nina off; Nina cried when she saw that Cohen had bought the child an ice-cream cone, and she was still crying as she waved goodbye from the boat.

When Cohen left Esther the Black on her parents' porch with chocolate running down her shirt, he returned alone to his lighthouse to grieve for Nina. He sat surrounded by dust and bourbon bottles for several days, and then he went back to the fishermen. He took Esther the Black with him, and she played in the dirt with the fishermen's children as Cohen found other lovers. But, he never stayed with one woman as long as he had stayed with Nina. That would not have been fair; he would not have loved any of them, he could not, because there was already Esther the White.

It was enough just to see her, Cohen told himself. It was enough to love her granddaughter as if the child had been shared between them. And each time he planted, lilies which surrounded the green lawn, a grove of mimosas which moved like a flock of Brazilian parrots outside her bedroom window, what grew was for her, for Esther. He took to having imaginary conversations with Esther the White, often about the upbringing of Esther the Black, which he felt was negligent. He imagined these conversations as he worked with his bucket and rake, clearing the poachers' remains off the beach.

It was just such a conversation Cohen was imagining the evening he stumbled upon Esther the White. Cohen climbed over the sea wall at the end of the day, he wiped his hands on his pale faded jeans to keep the salt from the blisters on his fingers and palms, and he buttoned his coat against the icy wind. He was thinking of how he would, if he could, tell Esther the White that they must send the kid away for the next summer. Last August, Esther the Black had been six, and children in the fishermen's camp began to work at that age; when the winter fell away, and school was through, the girl would be left with nothing to do. Maybe a gymnastics camp, Cohen thought as he loaded his bucket and rake into the tool shed, kicked away dead leaves and bits of rock, and lit a Marlboro. It was then that he saw Esther the White. She was in the pine grove. It was early winter, and Esther the White knelt in the ice and she dug in the earth in a place where the ivy refused to grow. Cohen could not move; he forgot his imaginary conversation, and he stood like a thief, hidden by the shadows of a large jutting stone in the sea wall, a place which would later become a break in the sandstone, a tear caused by freezing and melting ice. And Cohen himself was as still as a stone, as he watched the woman he loved paw at the earth like a white wolf or a witch.

Esther the White howled and cried; she wore a gray mohair coat and sunglasses, ivy was climbing up her coat sleeve. Cohen had been on his way to a poker game after work; he had intended to smoke cigarettes and watch the moon rise before he walked on to the fishermen's encampment. But, instead, he was still. Instead, he watched Esther the White. He crouched down low; he cupped the light of his cigarette in his palm. Esther the White was talking to herself as she dug in the earth. Her fingers were ringed and whiter than ice; the blue veins in her wrists shimmered and moved. Cohen had been that close to her. He had even seen her breath turn to smoke when it touched the air. And as Cohen listened he forgot everything but Esther's voice; he forgot the pain in his knee as he knelt in the ice, he forgot the salt on his own skin.

That winter, that evening, Esther the White had had enough. There, in the pine grove, the first week the family had arrived, she had hidden the cash and jewels she might some day need. For a time of emergency. She could cope with Mischa, and his brother, the dwarf; she had learned to accept Phillip's suicide attempts; she had barely noticed that fine lines had found their way to her pale skin. The real problem was that, at the age of forty-nine, she was pregnant.

Esther the White had stopped sleeping with Mischa years before they had reached New York, and the one time she had let him crawl into her bed, he had gotten her pregnant. She wanted an abortion, she needed an abortion. She had fallen for Mischa's line about an aching heart, she had let his cry of "Not long for this world" move her, and she had stared at the pale, beige ceiling as Mischa, her husband, who for years had not wanted to be bothered with the expense of a mistress, placed his penis inside her. And now she was pregnant. She had not even wanted Phillip, and she had been eighteen then. She clawed, in the frozen earth, until her fingernails were split; but she could not find the velvet jewelry box she had hidden. She found nothing; she had forgotten the spot.

Esther the White cursed her husband and his brother; she screamed out against her own parents. She wondered why she had ever been born. She had been forced to give birth to Phillip, who had tried to turn her into a shadow, a ghost, when he named his daughter after her, when he knew tradition forbade it. It was revenge, getting back at her because she had been a terrible mother, a mistake she would not make twice. But, most of all, Esther saved her rage for someone named Solo. When she spoke of Solo, Cohen covered his ears with his gloves. He ground his teeth, he shivered like a seagull. But, Esther the White did not stop, she cursed and she dug through the ice; she dug until her fingernails were black half moons; still, even with her fury to aid her, she could not find the buried money and jewels.

Cohen realized that he was beginning to know Esther better than he had ever known anyone before; he almost forgot his own memories, his travels, and years and blood. As she dug, Cohen imagined his own hands digging alongside of hers, dirt sticking to the blisters on his palms. And just then, as he was about to jump like a thief into the pine grove, as he was about to suggest that they get shovels from the tool shed and dig up all of the earth in the world if they had to, the fisherman appeared.

Cohen's friend, the fisherman he had met during his first night as guard, called out Cohen's name. The landscape artist was paralyzed; his bended knee was frozen to the earth. But Esther the White rose from the ice like a soldier. Her eyes were a terrible blue, her breath showed itself like fire in the frozen air. Cohen was terrified; he stared across the pines at Esther. If she told Mischa of Cohen's friendship with the fisherman, Cohen could be finished. He was supposed to be their guard, their enemy; he was not supposed to meet them for a game of cards on a winter's evening. He would be dismissed without pay, back to the city, jobless, without even a photograph of Esther the White.

But, quite suddenly, Esther the White moved close to the trunk of a tree and hid herself. The fisherman did not see her; he continued to wave at Cohen, to call out Cohen's name. Cohen was caught, a traitor in the Compound; but, before he could rise and face the music, walk over to Esther the White and be slapped or dismissed, Esther herself held a finger to her lips. Across the ice and the silence, in the instant that Esther held a finger in front of her lips, at the moment when Cohen slowly nodded back to her and agreed to be silent, the two had made a pact.

This is to be a secret, Esther wordlessly told Cohen; and, with her free hand, she waved him on to meet his fisherman. What Cohen did not understand then, when he did not know what was buried in the grove, was what Esther had to lose. Cohen wanted his job, and he wanted to be close to Esther the White. And if Esther had chosen to, she could have walked away from the pines, sipped Irish tea with lemon in her own warm kitchen, and casually mentioned to Mischa that she had seen Cohen with a fisherman, the enemy. What could Cohen have done to betray her? Whisper to her husband, "Listen, I saw your wife digging like a deer. It looked suspicious"? Mischa would only have answered, "So? This is her compound. What's it your business? I'm keeping an eye on you, busybody. Spy." Still, it had been Esther the White who first vowed a silence, who must have thought she had more to lose, although Cohen could not think of what that loss might be.

That night the moon rose, and Cohen walked away with the fisherman. He smoked cigarettes, played poker, drank a bottle of sweet wine, and made love to a woman with red hair. When he returned to his lighthouse, he slept dreamlessly; and when he awoke he was thinking of Esther the White. So, he returned to the pine grove early the next day. The morning was silent and cold, and already the earth which Esther the White had turned up had frozen solid. Cohen's fingers burned with cold as he spaded up the earth around many of the pine trees, and then carefully recovered the holes he had made. As he was about to give up, as the morning turned pale gray, his spade hit something between the roots of a small pine tree; he found a velvet jewelry box. He covered his marks, he looked over his shoulder. No lights were on in any of the houses, no footsteps fell on the earth, but still Cohen waited until he had returned to the lighthouse before he opened the box. Once home, he pushed the junk and clutter off his table; cigarette ash clung to his vest. Cohen lit a cigarette, and opened the box. Inside was newspaper. Cohen studied the newspaper; and then, slowly, he unwrapped the treasure Esther the White had hidden.

Cohen carefully examined one thousand dollars in cash, two tiny, delicate diamond earrings, and a polished stone as large as Cohen's own hand. The stone was jade, and carved into the jade was the face of a woman, her hair upswept, her nose delicate and fine. Around the stone was red gold studded with emeralds. In his hand Cohen now held more than he had ever earned, more than he would earn in a lifetime as a landscape artist. He couldn't bear to look at it, he couldn't bear to imagine what lover had given the jewels to Esther the White. So, he wrapped up the treasure and stared at the newspaper. All morning, he sat in the lighthouse and thought of reasons why Esther the White would hide a stone worth so much, and why she would now try to find it. He came to the conclusion that Esther the White was planning to run away from the Compound, and he must not allow that. But he could not keep the cash, he would feel like a thief. And, by the time he had walked down the Compound road to shovel the paths free of ice, Cohen had already decided to keep the jade pendant and the small diamond earrings; and before he went to speak with Esther the White, he sewed the gems into the lining of his sheepskin coat.

That night, he found her in the parlor of the main house. She sat on the couch, and Cohen hoped that her eyes could not somehow see through the lining of his coat.

"What is it?" Esther the White asked. She had been wondering if abortionists accepted American Express cards. When the bill came, she would try to convince Mischa that she had bought a new coat.

"Can we talk?" Cohen said. He shuffled his feet, and in his pockets his hands sweated over the dollar bills.

Esther the White had assumed that Cohen would not bother her; he would be thankful that she hadn't turned him in to Mischa as a traitor. "No," Esther said. "We can't. I'm thinking."

"Well, before you finish thinking," Cohen said, "maybe you could use this." He pulled the thousand dollars from his pockets and laid it alongside her on the flowery couch.

Esther the White stared up at him; she wondered how a man like Cohen could have so much money. And, although she was too polite to mention it, that was the first time she realized that he loved her. Esther the White folded the bills and stuffed them into her shoes. "A loan," Esther the White said, although she doubted that she could ever repay him; everything the family had was in Mischa's name.

Cohen shook his head. "What would I do with money?" he said. "Buy liquor? Spend a few days at Belmont betting on losers? Keep it."

They never discussed the money again; although it was Cohen who drove Esther the White to the abortionist's office in Forest Hills.

"I'm here for an abortion," Esther the White said as Cohen pulled up to the curb. "I thought I would tell you, so that you don't think anything's unusual if I look ill, so you don't mention anything to my husband."

Right then, Cohen wondered if he should tell her he had her jewels. His assumption must have been wrong; she seemed not to be planning to run away from the Compound. But he wasn't thinking fast, he was opening the door for her, and worrying about her going up to the doctor's office alone. And, before he knew it, he was alone in the car, Esther was gone, and it was too late to mention the jade pendant, too late to hold her hand.

Now as Cohen waited in the Cadillac, waiting for Esther and remembering how pale she had been after the abortion as they drove back to the Compound, Esther, too, thought of Cohen as she waited to be called by the nurse.

Esther the White did not bother to leaf through magazines like some of the patients; she crossed her legs, and, through the pocket of her cloth coat, she kept a hand pressed against her side. The air conditioning in the office chilled her pain until it was nothing but ice carving through her stomach. She pressed harder, and thought of Cohen, his rumpled shirt, his Russian accent, the way he drove Mischa's car, with one arm thrown across the back of the seat; he passed other cars too quickly, he was ready to turn down any one-way street. Esther the White could not remember having ever seen Mischa drive that car. But Cohen was dangerous; she must remember that. He knew too much about her, he had seen her years before, wailing like a wolf on the ice. And he was in love with her.

On either side of Esther, on the doctor's rust corduroy couch, patients sat anxiously. No one could know that Esther the White, wearing her gray linen coat in the heat of a July afternoon, was afraid of falling in love. She would have liked to open the door and wave to Cohen, to signal him to sit beside her on the couch and hold her hand, but it was too late; and when the nurse called out her name, Esther the White walked into the examining room, and she undressed and waited.

The doctor was young. Too young. Phillip's age, Esther thought, as she watched him read her medical records. Esther had visited the same doctor in the winter, when the pain began, and he had taken X-rays and blood tests; but Esther never returned, even though his office had sent her postcards which she had to tear into tiny pieces and flush down the toilet before Mischa could see them and guess that something was wrong. And now, as the doctor wrote in her file, Esther was thankful that Phillip had never become a doctor; who would want her son to become such a thing? Nothing but a death-dealer. It was better to try to drown every summer than to be able to smile at me this way, Esther thought, when he knows as well as I that it's death.

"You never returned for your follow-up," the doctor smiled. "That was childish."

Esther the White shrugged. She felt like a child, dressed up in a paper smock, her legs dangling from the cold examining table. She was glad that Cohen could not see her this way.

"We can't help those who don't want to be helped," the doctor said, after he had taken her blood pressure and her pulse, after he had listened to her heart and tapped every bone.

Esther the White could not remember if his name was Schwartz or Stein. It was suddenly important that she remember. "Schwartz?" she said, and the doctor nodded. "Dr. Schwartz," she said, "don't give me a runaround."

"Listen," Schwartz told her, "I'm not prepared to make a final diagnosis. We need further testing. Some consultations. Hospitalization. Without that, there's no way to know whether or not it's malignant."

"I don't need further testing," Esther the White said. "It's cancer."

"There is treatment," Schwartz said, but he was looking younger and younger to Esther all the time.

"Of course there's treatment," Esther said. "I know the treatment." She smiled. "Death."

"A biopsy first. And then, perhaps cobalt."

Schwartz filled out several prescriptions; but he promised more codeine and Demerol only if Esther the White would promise to set a date for surgery at St. Fredrics Hospital. Esther the White agreed; she agreed because she did not believe that she would last until the date they had set. She was doomed, and she knew it; but when Schwartz left her alone, Esther the White stared at her thin, pale arms and thought of Cohen. He had been a gentleman in the car, he had been a gentleman all these years, and now she wondered what it would be like to kiss him; she wondered if he could tell that her cells were crazy mutineers just from a touch of her tongue.

Esther the White dressed; she had thought that when the time came she could give it all up, with grace, with ease; but the pen slipped from her fingers as she filled out the index cards the nurse had left for her, and her hands were shaking. She grieved for all the years she had spent alone, without passion, between cold sheets, between dreams. She did not want to die; she wanted to kiss. And it was, she thought, too late for anything like kissing.

And it was much too late to reconcile with any of the family—Mischa had become used to sleeping without her, Phillip would never forgive her for his loveless childhood, the only one she might have a chance with was Esther the Black. And it was now or never; she did not have much time, and she wanted time to leave something, someone, behind, even if it might be too late for kisses and for sighs. She wanted Esther the Black, she wanted to take back all her cold glances and slaps; she wanted to sit in the dark and whisper all of her fears into an ear which would hold every word like a silver shell.

Esther the White buttoned her coat and walked through the waiting room, just as Cohen, outside in the Cadillac, was wishing that he could carry her away. Cohen was imagining touching her bare skin, as Esther left the doctor's office, carrying with her cells that could crush any kiss. Esther the White had made a decision. That was all there was to it; she would explain her life to Esther the Black, she would be forgiven and loved, she would leave someone behind. She walked to the open door of the Cadillac as she had walked when she was a girl, when the ice threatened to cover her, and she was forced to walk between the wolves. She nodded calmly to Cohen as he closed the door behind her, and she did not even bother to cry.

3

The same eelgrass had been moving in the same harbor for more than twenty years; and for all of those years Esther the White had watched the Compound from her bedroom window. Since she had discovered that she was ill, Esther the White had begun to feel more and more responsible; she was responsible for Phillip's suicide attempts, for Esther the Black's coldness. Lately, she had even begun to feel responsible for changes in the weather, for the falling tide, for storms which moved over the harbor, for rain. And she wondered if she had caused so much unhappiness around her because she had refused to allow her life to follow its predestined course; perhaps, she now thought, she had betrayed her sex, given up tenderness, any emotion at all, in a trade for control over her own life. Now, all of that control seemed wasted, and even her cells did whatever they pleased.

When she returned from the doctor's office, Esther the White cooked the Friday-night meal; the family would think it odd if she were absent. But she did not eat the pâté, she barely touched her melon, and she slipped two codeine pills onto her tongue before taking a sip of white wine. After dinner Esther the Black went to visit her father, who took all of his meals alone, carrying with her a plate of trout and rice, and Mischa and his brother Max took a long nighttime walk by the sea wall. Finally, Esther the White could go to her room, where she would stay, alone for the weekend, above the harbor where the eelgrass swam.

When the pain lessened, and the codeine moved through her blood in waves, Esther the White sat before a mirror, which Mischa had ordered from Italy; and, as she watched her motionless features in the glass, she could remember the first time she had made a decision. The month was October, and already snow had fallen, and already Esther the White, who had been named so because of her long white-blond hair, had begun to fear the wolves which they said lived above, in the mountains. Perhaps it was wolves that Esther was imagining as she pulled the strand of beads she was fastening around her mother's throat too tightly; when the strand broke, the beads, twenty yellow amber balls holding an enormous jade and emerald pendant, fell onto the wooden floor.

Esther the White was fifteen years old the day the beads fell and scattered beneath the furniture and between the floorboards. It was then, as Esther the White, too shocked to be anything but silent, watched the family's entire heritage and wealth roll this way and that on the floor, that her mother, a large woman who was too proud to be religious and who refused to wear a scarf over her head except in the coldest winter, announced that Esther the White was not her child.

"You didn't notice," the mother snapped, her face flushed red, as blotchy as borscht, "that you were the only one in this family with blue eyes and a black heart?"

Esther the White might have been struck dumb; the muscles in her face only twitched; her feet had rooted into the wood.

"You didn't notice," the mother continued, "that you were always lazy, that you were never any good. And that would not be if you were really my child."

Esther the White stared at the floor, at the crack in the floorboards where the jade pendant, which had been presented to the mother's grandfather by the Czar himself, had gotten stuck. She shuffled her feet as she was told that she had been taken in by the family as an infant, and that every family in town without a daughter adopted a girl infant or child. She was raised to inherit the laundry and the housekeeping, the cooking and the sorrow, and the kindling of the fire in the early morning when no one else would even think of getting out from beneath the mountains of blankets and quilts.

"Didn't you ever notice," the mother said, "that everyone in this town has a daughter? Even wives who are seventy years old have young daughters. How else can a house be kept clean? How else can a family be cooked for and fed?"

While the mother continued, listing Esther's faults, the girl began to think of escaping. She thought of other countries and other continents, though she had never been farther than their own frozen river. One of the young men in town had disappeared to a place called New Jersey. Another, who had been training to be a biblical scholar, now owned a chocolate factory and sent packages of clothing and sweets to his family from Paris. But Esther had heard most about New York, where it was easy to find work, to become rich and escape. Esther the White was trying to imagine what New York looked like; for when she began to gather together the scattered beads the mother beat her on the shoulders. It was with the thought of escape, with the thought of walking down the avenues in New York, that Esther slipped several amber beads and the huge carved jade pendant into her apron pocket.

When the mother counted the beads and found that six of the amber stones and the wonderful jade were missing, she slapped Esther's face and called her a liar. Esther insisted that the stones must have fallen beneath the floorboards, they must have fallen through a crack in the wood, and the pendant had disappeared into the snow. It was then, as she calmly lied, as her eyes stared innocently while the mother continued to scream and accuse until her breath was as short and wild as geese, that Esther the White decided that her unblinking eyes, which shone like river ice in February, were her best asset.

In that same winter, Esther discovered that she could see the reflection of her eyes in the river, even though the water was frozen with several feet of ice. She hunched over the riverbank, motionless as a wolf, and stared for hours, as if the proof to her mother's claim could be found somewhere behind her own eyes. She imagined other parents, who were tender and pale. She wondered if her mother had lied out of anger; but, when she stared at her own eyes, she was convinced that she was a gypsy or a queen or the child of a wolf, and her manner grew cool; she served dinner as if she were a captive, she avoided other girls in the village who giggled as they chopped river ice for drinking water, she refused the mayor's son the kisses she had once allowed him. She found herself dreaming about the jewels she had hidden in her pillow and the escape she would one day make.

It was at this time that their father began to beat Mischa, his oldest son. It was a long winter, and the rafts which floated lumber downstream to the city were locked in the ice; neither father nor son could work. There was not much to do in the village but argue and sigh. And the beatings began when the house grew tiny with winter, and snowdrifts reached the windowpanes.

"Why don't you leave this place?" Esther asked Mischa. But Mischa only shook his head sadly, and wondered what he might have done to anger his father, and Esther the White sighed, because she knew that to leave home and travel alone was dangerous for a girl. A girl traveling alone was suspect, a victim of the whims of border guards, innkeepers, and other travelers. So, Esther the White sighed and waited for Mischa to change his mind, and she was silent during the beatings, as was the younger son, Max, who would merely close his mouth over a spoon of beet soup when their father struck Mischa's head or back with his hand or a horse's whip. Max, himself, was never beaten. The parents called him the Baby; although he was three years older than Esther the White, he was tiny; his full-grown size was only four-foot-three. He was, although his parents would not admit it, a dwarf.

Esther the White neither liked nor trusted the Baby. She had the suspicion that talking to him might stunt her growth. She did not like the way his eyes flickered, or the children's clothes he still wore though he was eighteen. She avoided him. One evening Esther the White was turning a long wooden spoon in a pot of boiling potatoes, when the father began to strike Mischa. Mischa was silent and motionless; he was nearly twenty, and he was strong enough to ward off his father's anger; still he did nothing but look puzzled. Clearly he ached for his father's love. He did not know what his own sins might be, but Mischa could wonder forever, for what inspired his father's rage was only the long winter, the bad potatoes, the oily fish soup, the boredom. Esther the White let go of her wooden spoon; it floated in the whirlpool of the potato pot. It was time; and when the father had reached for his leather belt, which hung on a nail in the wall, Esther the White had already made her next decision.

It was easy; she was already at the stove. She simply held on to the iron handles of the pot which simmered beside the potato pot. Inside the smaller cauldron, chicken fat boiled; and Esther nearly stumbled before she reached the table, before the father had finished beating Mischa. It was then that Esther the White slowly poured the chicken fat over the father's head. The burning, boiling liquid fell onto his hair, onto the shoulders of his one good wool jacket. Chicken fat streamed through his beard.

"Bitch," he screamed.

The mother crouched on the floor, wiping at the fat, which was already turning to solid puddles on his boots, and she hissed at Esther from beneath her tongue.

"The bitch," he called again and again. He screamed. He held his hands in the air. He bared his teeth until they looked like fangs.

Esther the White held the empty pot by one handle, so that its bottom struck the floor like a gong as it swayed back and forth over the wooden floorboards. When the mother rushed the father out into the snow to cool his burns, she screamed to Esther that she would punish the girl in the morning, she would kill her, beat her until the leather belt was etched into Esther's skin. But Esther the White did not wait for punishment. That night, in the bed the three children shared, Esther whispered, "Now you have to get me out of here." Mischa was silent. The dwarf breathed between them, listening. "You have to help me," Esther said. "Because now they'll beat me or worse, just because I tried to help you, and I'm not even their daughter."

When Esther the White had lifted the pot above their father's head, she had counted on Mischa's guilt. But now he was more than guilty; he was afraid. He had shuddered when he saw the look in her eyes, as Esther had held the iron pot. He had not known her arms would reach that high, he would not have believed she could lift that much weight, he wondered if she was possessed.

"Not their daughter?" Mischa said. "Ridiculous." Between the blankets he shivered.

"Your mother told me," Esther said. "Do you think she's a liar?"

Mischa did not know. "Who are you?" he said to the girl he had known as his sister all his life.

"Someone who's not related to you, who just risked her own life for your well-being." She paused. "So, now you owe me your life. Now you have to rescue me. You have to do everything I tell you to do."

Mischa did not answer. He was a logger, as his father was, as his grandfather was. He tried to think of what might be beyond their village; he could only imagine ice, only an endless familiar landscape.

"Mischa," Esther hissed, and she was angry, furious that he was so silent and dumb when she needed a protector until the border was crossed. "Without you I am lost," she whispered.

They left before the moon rose. As soon as the father's cries ceased, as he finally stopped scratching the white cotton bandages which covered his burns, Esther filled a heavy woven sack with silver candlesticks and enough food for several days. She cut the jewels out of her feather pillow with a knife and slipped them into a secret pocket she had sewn in her coat. Esther the White smiled as she moved like a ghost through the dark, sleeping house. But Mischa moved heavily, slowly.

"Hurry," Esther the White whispered.

As Esther was slipping on her heavy coat, Max, the Baby, followed her. He was half-dressed, and struggling to pull on a small leather boot.

"What do you think you're doing?" Esther said.

The Baby smiled.

"Who said you could go with us?" she asked.

Max held a finger to his lips, and then he pointed to the closed door of the small room where the parents slept. He smiled.

"Blackmail," Esther the White said. When the Baby nodded, she shrugged. "All right," Esther said. "But hurry."

The night grew late. Soon the moon was high, and the ice was thick as walls. The parents slept beneath heavy blankets, the fire in the stove in the kitchen was nearly out, and the children walked quickly, on their way to the carriage house where Esther would pay for the journey over the border with three amber beads. By the time the stove in the kitchen went cold, the three had reached the border, their noses dripping, their skin turning blue, on a night too deep, too black for anything other than silence.

Later, the father would say they disappeared into the ice. He told the rabbi and the mayor of the town that now his only purpose in life was to find his children's remains, to see that a proper, religious burial took place. Whenever the bones of some wanderer who had strayed into the ice-blue winter, or the skeleton of a child who had fallen beneath the river were found, the father dressed in a long black coat and a fur-rimmed hat, and he walked with a line of mourners through the village. But to his wife he whispered: "May the ice eat them. May they get lost in the woods for a hundred years. May that bitch's eyes fall from her head, and her knees turn to stone."

When the father's hair refused to grow, when his skull remained totally bald from the scalding chicken fat, he told the villagers that the hair had fallen out because of the loss of his children. His scalp was so full of sadness that it could no longer hold a hair in place. But alone in his own house, at his own kitchen table, speaking to his own wife, he always wore a fur cap to hide his baldness, and he stroked his long beard, and cried hot tears into sugary glasses of tea, and he cursed Esther the White.

Two years later, Mischa, Esther, and Max were still in Marseilles, where they had arrived in the third month of their journey, having bought train tickets with money the pawned silver candlesticks brought. They had been caught in Marseilles by poverty; the brothers knew nothing of the jade pendant, and Esther the White had decided to save the jewel. Each time she opened the secret pocket in her coat for another amber bead, she stared at the carved jade until the anonymous woman's face in the stone became a friend, a loving secret, Esther's alone. And when all of the amber beads had gone for groceries and coal, Mischa got a job loading crates on the docks, in the hopes of earning passage money to England, and finally, to New York.

And so, for two years, Esther the White sat in a corner of the stable which the three rented, as far away as possible from the woolen blanket which separated them from the horses who shared their lodgings, whinnying and calling from the other side of the stable. Here, in a corner, Esther the White studied English. She had decided to ignore French, learning only enough to shop in a small market; she decided that they must change their family name, and she concentrated on learning English, perfecting her accent so that no one would ever accuse her of being Russian. Mischa protested when Esther the White crossed their original family name off all of their records, but she soon convinced him that it must be done so that their parents could never find them, when, in fact, Esther the White knew the parents would never want to find them.

After two years, Mischa still hadn't earned enough to get them out of France, Esther was still studying English by the small wooden window, the only window in their side of the stable. She wondered if she should, at last, sell the jade and emerald pendant, desert the brothers, and go off on her own. But she had an attachment to the pendant, she stared at it for hours when she was alone in the stable; and the one time she began to walk toward a jewelry store to have the gem appraised, two dockworkers followed her and pinched her arms and her breasts, until she turned and ran home to the stable.

Esther wondered if she would ever get to America, if she would ever have a plan, if she would have to wait forever. Then she noticed a small circus unloading its cages on the dock next to the loading platform where Mischa worked. That day, Esther the White knew, she had truly made a discovery.

The cages of the circus cried out each time Esther passed by them, as she carried Mischa his lunch. Slowly, Esther walked by the two silver greyhounds, the red-streaked monkeys, the lion with one eye, the Mongoloid idiot, the red-and-turquoise roosters, the turtle, the bear. On a Friday, when the circus had been in the city for nearly two weeks, Esther the White carried a bag containing Mischa's lunch—a sardine sandwich and two pears—but she walked no farther than the cage of the two-headed calf because suddenly there was someone behind her. When she turned she was looking right into the eyes of the tattooed man.

"Pardon," said the tattooed man, who had begun to stare at Esther the White's platinum hair.

Esther did not answer. She breathed deeply. The monkeys' eyes were dark brown; the silver greyhounds were silent.

"Excuse me. Very sorry," the tattooed man tried again.

He spoke English; his perfume was the odor of the sea. "Sorry," he said softly. "I might have tripped you. Clumsy." He laughed at himself.

Esther the White held the sardine sandwich tightly as she accepted the tattooed man's offer to see the circus cages. From his dock, Mischa watched as Esther followed the tattooed man, as she peered between the iron bars. When she had looked into each and every cage, Esther the White accepted the black cigarette the tattooed man offered her, though she had never before smoked, and did not inhale.

"Not bad for a little circus," she said.

"I am the manager," the tattooed man said. "The owner is an idiot. I practically run the circus."

"Not bad," Esther the White repeated. "But you could use more."

"Of course," the tattooed man sighed, staring at Esther's wide blue eyes. "Of course we could use more, who could not?"

"What you could use," Esther the White said, "is a dwarf."

"A dwarf?" the tattooed man said. "What for?"

"Attracts business." Esther the White eyed the monkeys, the fortuneteller who sat at the edge of the dock in flowing blue robes, the enormous fat lady who peered out at them from behind the sea turtle's cage. "Everybody loves little people."

"And everyone has also seen a dwarf."

"Not this dwarf," Esther insisted. "He is something special."

The tattooed man agreed to think about introducing Esther to the owner of the circus, a Pole named Jules. And Esther the White agreed to have dinner with the tattooed man, who bowed and introduced himself as Solo. Esther the White didn't have much time; soon the circus would be leaving France. In the next few days Esther shopped, spending all of Mischa's savings on Max. She bought him a silk shirt, a knitted cap, and dancing lessons from a Madame Laverne, who showed Esther her wiry blue varicose veins as if they were witness to the ballet career the Madame swore she had known. The three went without lunch and dinners, and ate only bread, cheese, and tea in the mornings. And no one dared to ask Esther the White why she now left her English grammar book in a messy heap of pages on the stable floor, or why she sang out snatches of English lullabies in the mornings, or why she had bothered to buy herself a pale violet dress when she had no place but the stable to wear it to.

But in fact, Esther the White wore the violet dress to a café; there was sawdust clinging to her shoes, and her pale hai hung to her waist. After they had eaten dinner, and Esther the White had decided that the tattooed man had the strongest face and most delicate hands she had ever seen, he surprised her by suddenly opening his hand. Inside his fingers, resting in his palm, quick as magic, were two diamond earrings. When Esther the White smiled and held the earrings to her ears, the tattooed man asked to sleep with her.

"But why would I sleep with you?" Esther the White asked. "I don't even know you. And, anyway, I've slept with two brothers all of my life."

The tattooed man explained that sleep did not really mean sleep. She could close her eyes if she wanted to, but never sleep. It was just a turn of phrase. An English phrase. What he really wanted to do was kiss her, make love to her, perhaps in the room he had rented across the street? He had given her diamonds, he found her charming, he was about to introduce her to the circus owner, Jules, with whom he had boundless influence.

"Do I look that desperate to you?" Esther the White asked.

The tattooed man was hurt, offended. "What makes you think this is just for me?" he said. And he told her about the tattoos which covered him, tattoos which swept women off their feet, forced them to knock at his door at midnight and at one. Parrots and red roses. Not pictures, but art, beauty. Esther the White considered. She was desperate; she had to meet the circus owner. But also, she admitted to herself, she was curious.

"Besides," the tattooed man, Solo, said, "it's such a friendly way to seal a bargain."

Esther shrugged. "Maybe," she said, as she clipped the diamonds to her earlobes.

He did speak wonderful English. The diamonds' sparkle reached across the room. Solo whispered that Jules might offer three hundred francs for a dwarf. Esther said she would not take less than three fifty.

"Follow me," Solo said.

Esther the White smiled. "Maybe," she said.

The diamonds held to her pale ears like glue as Esther the White followed the tattooed man up three flights of stairs in a rooming house. She watched the paintings on his skin appear as Solo removed his crimson shirt, his loose cotton slacks, the moccasins he wore. For a moment, standing in the draft which moved beneath the painted wooden door of the dark room, Esther wanted to disappear. To be back in bed, between the brothers, with the quilt pulled up high. But then she stared at the tattoos and she could not take her eyes off the colors. She forgot the brothers, she forgot her past, and she saw only the face of the man wearing a gold crown who stared out at her sadly from Solo's forearm, only the parrot, whose red claws stretched across Solo's chest, and the butterfly which flew up the calf of one leg.

He made love to her quickly, soundlessly. He pushed the violet dress up, and slipped off her underwear. Esther the White touched her fingers to the tattoos which ran across Solo's back.

Solo sighed then. "It's always this way," he said sadly. "They're always more interested in the tattoos than they are in me."

But, that was not true; Esther thought everything about Solo was wonderful. She did not even mind that the bed was metal and creaky, and that the sheets were torn and stained. Esther's eyes were open, Solo's were closed. He barely touched her at all, but Esther's fingers flew over his skin as if the tattoos were braille. She did not notice when he was finished. She didn't even realize that he had stopped moving inside her, until Solo said, politely, "I think we must go. I've only rented the room for an hour." Esther nodded; and it was only for a moment, as the tattooed man was slipping one arm into his shirt, that she thought of asking if she, and not Max, could leave with the circus. Then, she would no longer need to make decisions; she would simply follow the troupe, she would ride trains without ever knowing their destination, she would have time to record every tattoo that covered Solo's skin as they slept in the same bed each night. But she did not ask, she did not even mention the blood which ran between her legs; instead, she smoothed her hands over her pale hair, and she followed the tattooed man out of the rooming house, and past the crates of vegetables which lined the docks. There, they kissed good night, made arrangements to meet the following evening, and went their separate ways.

Each time Max took a dancing lesson with Madame Laverne, Esther the White met her lover, although she was careful never to wear her diamond earrings in front of the brothers. They rented the same room each night, and Esther the White would rub oil over Solo's skin and gaze at the tattoos, as Solo smoked pipefuls of opium. The seventh time they met, as Esther the White sat on the soiled bed without clothes, with only the diamonds at her ears, Solo told her that he had made an appointment for Esther and the dwarf to meet with Jules the following evening.

Esther the White did not know if she would laugh or cry as she walked down to the docks with the brothers. It was twilight; and Esther the White held the Baby's hand, as if he were a child or a pet.

"Where are we going?" Max said, and he had to yell so that his voice could be heard above the crying gulls that circled overhead.

"The circus," Esther told him. She wanted money and she wanted to go to America, she wanted never again to be someone's daughter or servant; but she also wanted Solo.

"There isn't a show today," Mischa said, repeating information he had heard just that morning on the docks. "They've given their last show here, and anyway, the bear has died."

Esther clapped her hands. "Oh good," she said. "Now that the bear's died, they will definitely need something new."

When she saw Solo, Esther left the brothers at the cages. There they waited, as the eyes of the animals, the monkeys and the silver greyhounds, grew yellow in the night. Mischa sat on the steps of the sea turtle's cage; his shadow fell through the bars, but the turtle did not move, she kept her gray eyes closed against the odor of the sea which rose around the dock. Solo was waiting for Esther with Jules, the circus owner, on the dock. Jules was interested in the idea of a dwarf, and Esther described Max's talents in flowing terms—but all the while she stared at Solo, who was leaning on a metal lamppost, cleaning his fingernails with a wooden match. When Jules had agreed to Esther's bargain, when he had handed her three hundred and fifty francs, the three walked to where the brothers waited. Esther walked slowly; each time she imagined the circus leaving, a thin line of pain wound itself around her forehead, like a ribbon, like a coil. When they reached the sea turtle's cage, Esther said to Max, "The owner would like to hire you."

"No," Mischa said.

"What would the salary be?" Esther asked Jules.

"Same as everyone else," Jules shrugged.

Esther noticed that one of Solo's shirt buttons was undone; she could see the outline of one red talon.

"And what does that mean?" Esther said. "Old bones, fish? Do you think my brother is a seal? A bear? He is a dancing dwarf. You must pay him a salary," she said. "Money," she demanded.

Esther and Jules argued over wages; Max cheered up when he heard how much Esther believed him to be worth, he puffed up his new knitted cap. "I don't come cheap," Max laughed, and then he asked the tattooed man to show him a tattoo. Solo lifted a hand lazily and pulled up his sleeve. A bluebird's wing covered his wrist, and Esther was afraid that if she turned to look she might faint.

Max was impressed with Solo's markings, but when the matter of a salary was finally settled, the Baby did not really want to go. He was afraid, even though Esther promised him that crowds all over Europe would pay to see him, they would applaud him, some might even bring him bittersweet chocolate-covered cherries—his favorite candy. Soon Max began to cry; Mischa stared morosely into the turtle's cage, afraid to contradict Esther, who continued to coax the Baby in her deep, chanting voice. That night, Esther the White spoke to Max more than she had in a lifetime, she was not about to have the dwarf wreck her plans, especially when Solo did not even look at her, did not even smile; so Esther held Max's hands, and she whispered, soothingly, for hours.

Finally, they retired to Jules wagon, where they sat on velveteen pillows and drank glasses of sherry to seal the bargain.

"Come on," Jules said to the Baby, "cheer up. You'll be like my own son."

Max was too tired to argue or cry; Esther patted him on the head, and nodded to the circus owner.

"Though to tell you the truth," Jules confided, "I could use a watchdog more than a son. I've got a thief around here. I can't rest in peace. Even my dead wife's jewelry isn't safe. All I had were earrings to remember her by, and now," he clapped his wrinkled hands together, "they're gone."

Esther the White touched her naked ears, and looked over at the tattooed man.

Solo had drunk five small glasses of sherry, and now he smoked a pipeful of opium. As Esther the White watched, he rested his head on a maroon pillow and closed his eyes. She wondered, now, if she knew him at all. His eyes remained closed when Esther the White stood over him and softly said goodbye. He did not answer; he may have been asleep, or in a soft, white dream. Esther the White looked around the wagon, and wished that she were a fortuneteller, that she wore a blue turban tied around her head. She wished that she could climb over the velveteen pillows and cradle Solo's head in her arms. And she might have; if Solo had said one word, if he had even opened his dark eyes, but he did not move. So, Esther the White licked her lips and turned away; she had no time to waste; she was on her way to America, to riches. She had a plan and a timetable; and anyway, the tattooed man was sleeping, so he could not have asked Esther to go away with him, even if he wanted to.

When Esther the White and Mischa left the wagon, Jules was searching through a trunk for a nightgown which would fit Max; Solo was snoring lightly. It was nearly dawn, and, when they walked past the docks, Mischa could see that the silver greyhounds were really the shade of dust in the morning light, and that they were nearly starved. As soon as they were away from the docks, Esther the White tried to erase Solo's dark, dreaming eyes; she could hide the stolen earrings away, she could hide the memory of Solo as well. She raised her pale eyes and pinched Mischa's hand. "We're almost there," she whispered. "We can leave for England. We'll be in New York before you know it."

They stayed in France only a few more months. Slowly, Esther the White realized that she was in love with Solo; she could not erase him; but it was too late. Esther often returned to the dock where the circus cages had stood; the troupe had disappeared, and no one who worked the docks seemed to know where they had gone. And even if Esther the White had discovered where the tattooed man was, she might not have followed him. Long ago, as she peered into the frozen river, she had decided not to let anything get in the way of her plans. And so, she stopped going to the dock, she stopped staring into the dirty water; and although she often dreamed of Solo, and found that she was holding on to nothing but air in her sleep, Esther the White and Mischa had become lovers.

She surprised Mischa one night by holding her arms around him just as he had begun to dream. Mischa touched her hair, imagining that Esther might suffer from nightmares, as he did. But, Esther the White slipped off her woolen nightdress, and asked to be held closer still, hoping that someone else's arms, anyone else's arms, would help her to forget Solo. Mischa fell in love, Esther the White did not; although sometimes, at night, while Mischa slept, Esther would lightly touch his face, and wonder if she should have left him behind, in their village. And Mischa moved somewhere between delight and guilt; wondering if there was some unspeakable thing wrong in what they did, wondering if he didn't love Esther a little too much, for they always made love in the dark, like strangers who have met accidentally. Often their own breathing was mirrored by the horses breathing behind the blanket—softly and hidden behind the wool room divider, but breathing all the same.

They left Marseilles in the spring. By the time they reached England, two months after Esther the White's eighteenth birthday, she was already pregnant with Phillip. Mischa found work, this time as a housepainter and carpenter, and soon he had earned enough to buy a small flat. He studied English; although when he dreamed of his brother, Max, the same sad dream, almost every night, he dreamed in Russian or French. Soon after they had moved into the flat, Mischa asked Esther, who now spoke perfect English, to marry him.

Esther the White still imagined the tattooed man each time they made love, and she kept the diamond earrings he had given her in a secret jewelry box which also held the stolen jade pendant. But she was now five months pregnant and she didn't know if the father was the man who stood before her, or if he was the man who had turned out to be nothing more than a thief. So she smiled and said yes, having decided that since they were not really brother and sister, to be married would not be anything at all like a sin.

4

Esther the Black knew nothing of her grandmother's history. Through the girl's lifetime, Esther the White had barely nodded through the pale walls which surrounded her, she had barely spoken to Esther the Black. Any words which were spoken were instructions or criticisms, as quick and as cold as ice. By the time she was six, Esther the Black already knew that she was not what her grandmother had hoped for. She was not blond, she was not cool, she did not hold her knife correctly, she cried. The two had nothing in common: only their name—that, and Phillip.

Esther the Black had been raised to fear her grandmother.

Her own mother, Rose, believed the only way to inherit the family's money was to train her daughter to behave. And to behave was to fear. Rose had grown up in Bridgeport, and she still stood at the sea wall and searched the ghostly coast of Connecticut for her home town, though she had not been back for years. Rose had discovered Phillip in a business course at N.Y.U. which Mischa had demanded he audit. The family had just arrived from London, the Compound was not yet finished, it was only sand and stone, and Phillip and his parents had sublet an apartment on East 79th Street.

"Temporarily," Phillip had told Rose. "We move around quite a bit."

His accent was English, his eyes were golden, his family was rich, and Rose was twenty-six and still unmarried. She aspired to better things and places than Bridgeport, Connecticut. So, Rose seduced Phillip on the bathroom floor in his parents' apartment, and four months later they were married in an Episcopalian church on 62nd Street.

When Rose's Connecticut family discovered that the family had Anglicized their name, and had once been Jewish, they stopped telephoning, they stopped talking. And when Phillip began hovering near the banks of the East River, Rose was actually relieved that Esther the White suggested that the family move into the completed Compound, which already showed sure signs of failure, since not one house had been occupied or bought. They would move in, Esther the White insisted. Temporarily. But, after two years, when not one of the pink houses had yet been bought, and Rose now had to care for a year-old daughter who looked nothing like herself, and a husband who attempted suicide each pale, gray summer, Rose began taping pictures of the desert onto her bedroom wall.

It was difficult, but Rose soon learned to ignore Esther the White's cold stares when she poured herself gin and tonics in the morning, when she hummed and decorated Esther the

Black's nursery with mobiles of cactus flowers and slot machines. Esther the Black had, in fact, been conceived as a gift to Esther the White. Rose had imagined that if she brought forth an heir, the old bitch would get off her back, retract her cold stares, and set up a trust fund. But, Esther the White did none of those things; she refused to see the child for several days, and when she learned that Phillip had named the girl after her, she was taut with hysteria, frightened of having her name stolen, of becoming a ghost. So, Rose gave up. She stopped trying to please Esther the White, but she insisted her daughter try even harder. Rose's passion for Nevada sprung up at the same time she began to despise Esther the White, the family, and everything about the Compound, even the sea. Her desire for another state grew obsessive. And when Esther the Black was older, Rose dressed her like an Indian with a rouge-painted face each and every Halloween. She drove the girl out to the new tract housing which had begun to circle St. Fredrics; and, from the driver's seat of Mischa's Cadillac, Rose watched as her Indian daughter gathered Almond Joys, sour balls, and apples.

In 1962, Rose begged Mischa for a TV, which she said would be therapeutic for Phillip—a connection to the real world. But Phillip refused to desert his *National Geographics*, and Rose alone watched TV. She tuned in to game shows each morning, practicing the quizzes, and dreaming of the time when she would rise like a storm from the audience and then—from podium or chair—she would win the cash she needed to fly off to Nevada; if she were lucky she might win a Camaro as well, perhaps a year's supply of groceries, or unlimited stays in Best Western Motels. And although she never appeared on a game show, never even went so far as to take the ferry to Manhattan, she did make it to Las Vegas, once.

Rose charged all of her expenses on an American Express card she had stolen from Mischa's kidskin wallet. The day that Rose left, Esther the Black was in school, and the TV reception was hazy because of a spring rainstorm. After finishing her last bottle of tequila, Rose decided that she could not face another Drowning Season.

Phillip still referred to her flight as the "Nevada Caper"; the rest of the family tightly named it "Rose's Episode." Esther the Black was listening at the door when Phillip persuaded Esther the White to convince Mischa not to press charges, to let Rose return to the Compound—even though she had been apprehended by a policeman in the lobby of the Dunes, where she had run up an eight-hundred-dollar tab in a week.

"Darlings," Rose had whispered to Phillip and Esther the Black, after her return, after Esther the White had coolly appraised Rose's tanned arms, "I'm awfully sorry about the mess. But, really, my life's as dry as instant potatoes. And it's your mother," she pointed a sun-browned finger at Phillip, "who keeps us here."

But Rose could not and would not leave. She had stayed so long, she would stay a bit longer, at least until Phillip received the inheritance which she would manage. And now, fifteen years after the Nevada Caper, it was Esther the Black who dreamed of escape. It was Esther the Black who guarded her eyes whenever anyone in the family demanded to know her plans for the future, it was Esther who wore her denim cap so that no one would have the chance of peering into the ideas which moved inside her skull. Rose had tried to frighten Esther the Black into behaving, but it hadn't worked. "Penniless," Rose would hiss, when Esther the Black despaired over Ira Rath, or her lack of friends, or the criticism which was showered down on her by Esther the White.

Rose had had a lifetime of dust, a lifetime of waiting for an inheritance which was being bled by Phillip's analysts and clinics, and Esther the Black had no such fears. She knew from the fishermen that there was nothing frightening about sleeping in shacks and eating rice and beans with sweet fish sauce. There was only one threat which kept Esther the Black in line, which kept her at the Compound and forced her to sit up straight when she wanted more than anything else in the world to slouch: she was afraid that any slip-up of her own would reflect on her father.

"They'll throw him in the loony bin," Rose would whisper when Esther the Black would not take her vitamins or smile. "They'll say he's a bad influence on you. They'll lock him up for good, and cut our allowances in half."

Of course, there was more to fear. To leave the Compound, and then to be forced to return—through bad luck, or bad vibes, or a bad tuna-fish sandwich that produced ptomaine and stacks of hospital bills which Esther the Black could never afford. Endless scenarios rushed through Esther the Black's skull whenever she thought of escape; in each she was driven to her knees, forced to return to the Compound as more of a prisoner than ever before. She was a maid, a chauffeur, Cohen's assistant, a sharecropper struggling to pay off the debts incurred during her short visit to the outside world. And always, in every scenario, it was Esther the White who was the guard, Esther the White she had to pay back. All in all, Esther the Black was scared. She feared that someone in the family would discover that she had a job, or that she hid all of the money she earned beneath her mattress; they would know that she planned to take her parents and leave, disappear, into the bright Nevada sun.

Esther the Black was afraid of her own plan; perhaps because she dared not even tell Cohen, who had always been her ally; but she needed to talk, she needed support. That may have been why, in the third week of July, she telephoned Ira Rath. She telephoned from the only Compound phone, which was located in the entrance hallway of her grandparents' house. She called to ask the accountant's son, whom she had not seen since he first went away to his college in Vermont, if he would be her accomplice; and she quickly found the number, listed under Solomon Rath on West 87th Street.

"Ira?" she said, turning to glance over her shoulder, freezing whenever a floorboard creaked.

"His father," the voice said. Esther the Black stopped talking. The accountant might know her voice; she had seen him at Friday-night dinner less than a month before. "You want my son?" Solomon Rath asked.

"Yes," Esther said quickly, disguising her voice. "I'm a friend from school."

"He doesn't go to school anymore," the elder Rath sighed. "He dropped out of Bennington at the end of his last semester. A friend from school would know that. Who is this?"

Esther the Black panicked. It was early morning, she would be late for work, Esther the White would glide down the staircase in her pale blue robe and find Esther the Black, a traitor at the phone. "All right," Esther the Black said to the accountant. "The truth is I'm in love with your son. I've seen him in Central Park." Esther had been to Manhattan only twice in her lifetime, and then just to visit Phillip in Doctor's Hospital the summers he contracted pneumonia; but she had seen enough movies on Rose's TV set to know that the park was a place for lovers. "I followed him home. That's how I got your name and address. I must talk to him. I must."

She waited. The accountant breathed. "So," he said, "it's you." He moved his mouth away from the phone. "Ira," he called. "It's Esther the Black on the phone."

Esther lit a cigarette and wondered how Rath had known her. Did she have a reputation for craziness? Had her grandmother warned the accountant, as they pored over the family's financial records together in his air-conditioned office, that Esther the Black was capable of anything, that she might telephone at early hours of the morning, lying and proclaiming a false love?

"Hello." It was Ira; he had been asleep, his voice was thick, a stranger's.

"Don't say a word," Esther told him. There was silence on the other end of the phone. Esther stubbed out her cigarette without having ever inhaled. "Good," she nodded. "We have to get one thing straight. I feel I have to tell you that I don't intend to marry you. So forget about it."

"All right," Ira said. And then he asked, "Who is this?"

"Esther. Esther the Black. Now, don't say a word. I may need your help. I assume that, as a childhood friend, you will oblige me."

"What the hell," Ira said. "We've known each other for a long time. Of course I'll help you. If we had married we would have been divorced. Of course, then I would have had alimony, some sort of settlement. I'll be damned if I know how to get the money to cut a record. But I've gotten a band together, and I'm not too proud to take The Quick and the Mad into every sleazy bar in New York if I have to."

"I would have paid you alimony?" Esther the Black said.

"Sleazy bars," Ira Rather repeated, "are the price you pay when you love rock and roll."

"Rock and roll." Esther shrugged. She was confessing her secrets, and he spoke of music.

"I'm a singer. A personality. That's why I dropped out of school. My father okayed it because he figured I'd be taken care of with your family's money. But to hell with your money, Esther the Black. To hell with it. And to tell you the truth," he lowered his voice, "my father says there really isn't a financial reason for our marriage anymore. He says if your grandfather doesn't sell off some property you'll all be in the poorhouse."

"Don't say another word," Esther warned. "Someone may be listening."

"Nah," said Ira Rath. "Esther the Black, what hell our marriage would have been." He sighed.

"I don't know," Esther the Black said, insulted, and suddenly shy.

"But my father would sooner have me dead and buried

than playing rock and roll, even if that means marriage to you," Ira said.

Esther the Black and Ira agreed to mislead their families; they would be co-conspirators, they would meet like lizards in a cheap bar at the harbor of St. Fredrics. It was a relief for Esther to finally whisper her plans of escape to someone. But then Ira Rath nearly ruined it all by lowering his voice and saying, "If we're really going to be allies, you have to confide in me. Are you a virgin? I could never relate to virgins."

"Ira," Esther the Black said. "That's none of your business."

But it was too late; he had forced her to think about the fishermen. Esther the Black rubbed her forehead and remembered. If she hadn't been the Drowned Man's daughter, some fisherman might have asked her to run away with him, to the Florida Keys, to Miami, or she might have moved into some young man's camper and learned how to repair fishing nets.

Esther the Black had never had friends in St. Fredrics, and Ira Rath had been nothing more than an occasional visitor who wore blue suits and glasses and taught her to smoke cigarettes. She had only the fishermen's children; and when the fishermen's girls her age began to wear bluejeans and shawls, when they kissed any boy who was interested, Esther the Black sat with them on the cold stone beach. The winter when she was sixteen, Esther decided that it was time for her to have a lover, and she chose a boy named Terry, perhaps because she had known him all of her life, perhaps because he had his own tent, which he heated in the winter with a small coiled electric heater that he plugged into his older brother's trailer with a stiff extension cord. Esther the Black often jumped out of her window at night, and slid off the roof, while Phillip and Rose slept beneath an electric blanket on the first floor. It seemed natural to Esther for her to fall asleep in that tent; even when the snow was falling, when the Compound paths were icy; she felt safe, and miles away from her grandparents' house. But in a few weeks, Terry began avoiding her. Finally, one day when she went with Cohen to help scale fish in the encampment, Esther the Black confronted him.

"What's wrong with you?" she asked the boy. "I'm not pregnant you know," she whispered as Cohen called for hot coffee and a pair of gloves to protect his fingers as he scaled half-frozen fish.

Esther the Black watched her lover all day, and when she accidentally touched his shoulder, as she helped a group of young men carry boxes of fish to a pick-up truck, Terry pushed her hand down. "Get away from me," he said, looking over his shoulder, as if afraid that one of his friends might see them touch. "Esther the Black, please go away."

Esther the Black ran. Her feet slipped on icy paths. She ran until her breath filled the air; and then she collapsed, in a dark flower bed beneath the first-floor window of her grandparents' house. She wore an old raccoon coat which had once belonged to Rose; the shoulders were padded, like armor. She pulled her legs up, the flowers all grew beneath her, underground. Terry had followed, and he appeared suddenly beside her in the flower bed where there was only ice, and not even the movement of one leaf.

"Sorry," Terry said, and Esther the Black shrugged; she did not think she would climb out her window at night to meet with him again. "Do you love me?" he then asked her.

The flowers grew underground, and Esther the Black wondered if she would ever love anyone. If she said yes, I do love you, would Terry be crazy enough to feel guilty, to run away with her? Would he, palms coated with the harbor salt and ice, rescue her and give her a life?

Esther the Black lit a cigarette; the fisherman's blue headband was dark navy colored in the night, and he looked around, over his shoulders, into the ice and the darkest trees, and Esther the Black then realized that Terry had never before been to this section of the Compound, to her section. She wondered what her grandmother would say if she wandered out onto the porch to breathe some winter air and saw a poacher in her flower bed; she wondered if her grandfather, Mischa, would raise his walking cane if he saw that the fisherman's fingers were now touching her skin. "No," Esther the Black said finally, "I don't love you."

The fisherman smiled and tossed a stone into the snow. "I was worried about that," he said as he moved his arms to surround her padded shoulders, and he smiled beautifully, as if Esther the Black had just released him. Each time Esther the Black saw her fisherman in the encampment after that time, after he had run off into the darkness, he smiled sadly. And Esther paid him back for following her into that most dangerous section of the Compound, her section, by never mentioning his name to any of the girls her age. After that, Esther the Black was sure the fishermen and their children were afraid of her; she was an outsider, and they would never trust her. She began to stay away; she went so infrequently to the fishermen's campground that even Cohen had grown suspicious.

"Esther the Black," he said to her, "tell me, do you have a boyfriend in town?"

Esther the Black rolled her eyes.

"I never see you in the campground."

"I'm busy," Esther lied.

"Too busy for old friends like the fishermen?" Cohen had asked.

"Yes," Esther the Black had said, but she was thinking of her fisherman's dark eyes, and the way his breath moved in the deep, frozen air, and the way he whispered to her in the night. "Too busy."

When she had stayed away for months, when Cohen tried to explain her absence with half-hearted excuses, the fishermen grew to believe that Esther the Black had deserted them for her own family, as they had always suspected she would; they began to avoid her on the streets of St. Fredrics, on the roads, and the beach. The girls she had grown up with got married—they had children, they worked on the fishing boats or as waitresses in town. Sometimes, Esther the Black would watch them from the sea wall; women who wore their hair long and wild, tied with the thinnest of blue headbands, working on the boats as their children waited, patiently, among the green stones, on the beach. She was not certain which of them her fisherman had married, but Esther the Black was certain that woman would wear her hair to her waist and never count her hours in the sun.

But now Ira Rath was still breathing over the phone, and Esther the Black heard a footstep on the stair. "Friday," Esther the Black said. "Don't forget."

She hung up the phone and ran out the door of her grandparents' house. She hitched a ride to town on Route 16, and that day, as she sold forty dollars' worth of eye make-up, and sixteen dollars' worth of blush-on rouge, Esther thought of Ira Rath. It was great luck that he wasn't interested in marrying her, that he hadn't pleaded with her to keep their engagement; and yet, she was disappointed. He had thought of her only as a step on the road to stardom. He had never really been her friend, Esther the Black decided; and, by the end of the day, she was no longer certain she wanted him as her ally.

Esther the Black locked up her register and walked to the soda fountain at the front of the store. She did not realize that Cohen was there until she was already seated at the counter; then she looked the other way. She had always trusted Cohen before, but her escape from the Compound was too important, and each time she tried to talk to him about Esther the White, he told her not to be disrespectful. So Esther the Black quickly ordered a lemonade. She stared straight ahead, at the menu which hung above the grill. The overhead fan moved in heavy circles. Though she loved him, Esther the Black wished that Cohen would go blind. She couldn't risk her grandmother's anger if Cohen should spill the beans. And she wished that he would go blind instantly, at the Woolworth's soda fountain. As customers and waitresses gathered around the blinded Cohen, Esther would skip right past him, out to freedom, out the door.

"Over here," Cohen called from his stool at the far end of the counter. "Esther, over here."

Esther the Black picked up her glass of lemonade; her straw bobbed like a pigeon. She still wore her pink smock, with ESTHER embroidered over her right breast. She sat next to Cohen but did not look at him.

Cohen pointed to his steaming porcelain cup. "Tea," he told Esther. "Because I'll tell you right now, coffee in a place like this is death."

"Cohen." Esther the Black clamped her teeth down on the striped straw between her lips. "Don't tell anyone that you caught me."

Cohen sipped tea. "All right," he agreed.

They sat in silence, the overhead fan droning, flies landing on the polished counter top.

"Don't tell anyone I caught you doing what?" Cohen asked.

"That you found out I'm working here." Esther the Black pointed to her pink smock. Cohen had not missed Esther the Black, he had not guessed she had found a job; he was waiting for Esther the White, who had locked herself in her room for days after the doctor's appointment. Finally one hot afternoon, she had come out to sit on the wide porch with a cup of jasmine tea resting on her knee; but she had stared right through Cohen when he walked past on the green, and her eyes were so heavy and so huge that they were closed and dreaming in the sun, and Cohen was left to imagine hundreds of ailments and diseases that Esther the White was too proud to mention.

Cohen glanced at Esther the Black. "Very pretty," he said of the smock.

"And whatever happens, don't tell my grandmother."

Cohen frowned and shook his head. He had been the one

to introduce Esther the Black to gardenias, to tea boiled from orange lilies, to the dozen sorts of seaweed and grass which grew in the harbor. And now, she thought only of leaving after he had taught her so much; and there was no way to tell her that he thought she misjudged her grandmother, without letting the girl know too much of his secret, too much of his love. "No one will hear your secrets from me," Cohen told Esther the Black. "Suddenly you don't trust me?" He shook his head.

Esther the Black was silent; she sipped at the last of her lemonade.

Cohen rose from his seat. "Let's go," he said. "Even the tea here is bad."

Esther the Black followed Cohen out to the street where Mischa's Cadillac was parked. She leaned deep into the maroon leather. They drove down Route 16 with all the windows open. She looked over at Cohen as he stopped the car to let two deer cross the road; she studied his face, the wrinkles, the lines.

"I'm sorry," Esther the Black said; she patted his hand. "I trust you," she said.

Now it was Cohen who felt like a traitor; he wondered how the girl would react if he told her that he loved her grandmother; that he had always loved her. He watched as Esther the Black lit a cigarette, then he started the Cadillac down the road and he thought, What a shame. I love her like a granddaughter, but what a shame she doesn't take after her grandmother at all. The hot afternoon wind moved through the car, from window to window, and no long blond hair flew out into the air; instead, Esther the Black's short dark hair rested in motionless curls as she puffed on her cigarette. Still, she was a good kid; she was smart, Cohen thought; perhaps she had inherited that from Esther the White.

"What's she like?" Esther asked over the wind.

Cohen stepped on the gas. Was the girl able to read his mind? Perhaps they had spent too much time, too many years together. "Who?"

The afternoon was at its latest; clouds moved in the sky; and Esther the Black wondered what Esther the White would say when she awoke one morning to find that all her prisoners, Phillip and Rose, and Esther, herself, were gone. "My grandmother," Esther the Black said.

Cohen laughed. "Why ask me? You're the relative. How should I know? You think I'm magic? You think I know everything?"

"I was just interested," Esther the Black said, as she slipped off her pink smock and crumpled it into the large leather bag she carried. "I wanted the opinion of an outside observer."

Cohen stomped down on the gas pedal after they rounded a curve on the road. He considered himself an observer, but not outside, never outside. "You don't know what you're talking about," he said to Esther. "Maybe you're suffering from overwork."

They entered the iron Compound gate; and as soon as the Cadillac drove onto the path, the odor of honeysuckle fell like a curtain. It was the beginning of twilight, the time when the Compound was its sweetest. "You talk nonsense, Esther," Cohen said. "You always want to leave, but you've got such beauty here, and you don't even see it. That's the word of this outside observer."

Esther the Black looked up, and agreed; the lighting—which could turn the branch of a tree bright and then dark in seconds—was beautiful at this time of day. Along with Cohen, she stared at the fading rose-colored houses, those the family lived in, and those which had never been anything but empty and which were now swept with pale sand and tiny green crabs. It was so cool and quiet, as the beginning of an evening fog moved over the Compound, that Esther almost forgot why she wanted to escape. And when Cohen stopped the car in front of her grandparents' house, Esther the Black was remembering the time Cohen had taught her how to press sea lavender between glass. She smiled over at him, she trusted him completely, but Cohen was looking away, he was looking at the harbor.

"Esther," he said, "look."

The family was gathered at the sea wall. Mischa, who stood six-foot-one, and his brother, Max, who was dressed in a boy's flowered bathing suit, both waved frantically at the harbor. Behind them stood Max's wife, Lisa, holding a beach towel. Rose had already climbed atop the wall; she waved clenched hands, as if she were praying into the dull, gray air. They were all calling together; but it was the time when the gulls and the pipers shared the air with the sparrow hawks and owls, and Esther the Black couldn't hear their words. The shadows which fell onto all of the porches grew longer now; the blood sea star and the snail moved in the harbor.

"It's your father," Cohen said. "It's Phillip."

Cohen opened the car door, he ran to the sea wall. The others remained, calling and waving, as Cohen reached the place where the earth suddenly turned to sand. He climbed over the stones, almost as if he were a young man; over the algae, the barnacles, the rust. And when Cohen scrambled over the stones on the beach, the spell was broken; the others began to move. Mischa unlocked the sea-wall gate, and then he and Rose untied the rowboat, as Max jumped up and down, excited as a child.

When Esther the Black sat down in the white wicker chair on her grandparents' porch, Cohen was already kicking off his shoes, diving into the water, and chasing after Phillip, who, once more, had followed some old sea-wish down into the harbor. Esther the Black rocked back and forth in her chair; Drowning Season had become a part of her internal clock. She wondered if she would even exist in another place, if her plans of escape were worthless. She stared at the stone beach, where the gills and tails of bluefish and flounders the fishermen had caught moved without power, until the gills were quiet, the tails calm. Esther rocked back and forth; she had watched a drowning every summer of her life; and she watched again now, as Cohen's arms encircled her father.

The Compound was dark, except for a flame across the lawn, where a blue gas fire that Lisa had forgotten to shut off heated a copper kettle. Esther the Black was staring at the blue light when Esther the White came out to the porch. Out there, in the harbor, Mischa had begun to row toward the circular current where Cohen lifted Phillip's head above the tide. Esther the White wrapped a woolen sweater around herself, and still she was chilled, she was cold as ice as she stared out to the lights of Connecticut. Max was now screaming instructions as the rowboat weaved crazily through the harbor—Mischa hadn't gained control over the oars. And Cohen waited patiently, holding Phillip's head above the waves, as Esther the Black's father stared upward, at the still, gray night.

Esther the Black rocked back and forth, she rocked faster. Although she knew her grandmother stood behind her, she did not want to turn. Esther the White watched her granddaughter's shoulders, she watched the dark, tight hair, as if the girl were a statue. Alien. A head carved in stone, in Greece or in Spain, centuries before. Stone that would not turn even when Esther the White breathed into the girl's hair, and wished as hard as she could that Esther the Black would turn to her. Esther the White ignored the harbor, where her husband rowed toward Phillip and Cohen; she watched her granddaughter, thinking that if they were not such strangers the girl might hold her, and then the chill might disappear; and then Esther the White felt foolish. She straightened her back and stood behind her granddaughter's chair.

"Fools," Esther the White said, looking out into the hazy harbor. It might have always been a mistake to fight Phillip; perhaps they should finally let him have his way, let him float peacefully into the soft sand at the deepest part of the harbor. "Always bringing the same drowned man back to shore," Esther the White sighed.

Slowly, Esther the Black nodded; they should let him be, she thought, as she watched Phillip struggle in the waves, in the dim moonlight. The girl stared out at the night harbor, and she felt her grandmother run her pale, thin fingers across the back of the chair as if the wicker were skin. Esther the White was wishing that they could both stop holding back their tears, but they were silent, their eyes were dry. And the two women watched the family come to shore on the other side of the sea wall; on the dark porch, between the shadows and the stones, together they watched the rescue.

II. NATURAL HISTORY

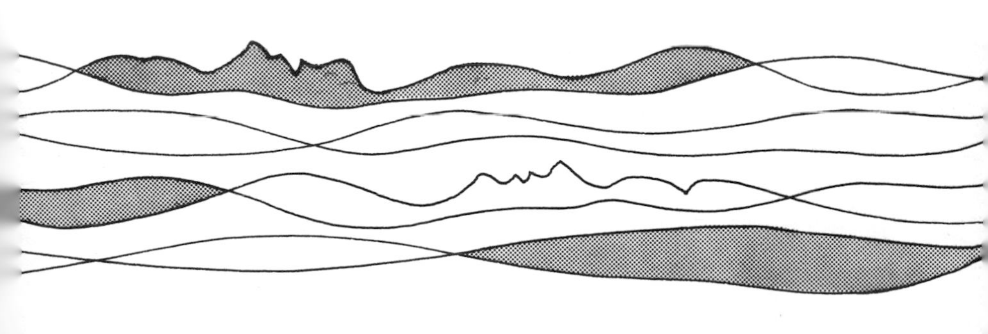

1

Each summer, after Phillip's drowning, the family sighed with relief. Everyone hoped that he would make the attempt early in July, so that for the remainder of the summer the watch could be relaxed. It was a fact that Phillip drowned only once a season, once a year. He was predictable. And afterward, his dosage of Valium could be reduced, and the family no longer shuddered each time the tides changed, each time the odor of seaweed and clams drifted over the lawn. Only Esther the White felt no relief; for this summer, after the drowning, she began to dream, nearly every night, of her son.

Often, in her dreams, Esther the White saw her own pale hands slipping her infant into the hands of Inge, the nursemaid, fluent in German and English, who had taken care of Phillip in London. On the night of the drowning, perhaps because of the pain in her side, perhaps because of the codeine, Esther the White dreamed that she had never wanted her son born. For years, Esther the White had forgotten that when she learned she was pregnant, her first reaction was to greedily eat the skin of young onions, for unmarried girls in her village had whispered about the use of onions as a spell against unwanted pregnancy. Even after her marriage to Mischa, when her stomach had begun to swell, Esther the White had sat for hours in hot baths, so that the steam might enter her, find its way to her womb, and suffocate Phillip. Her breasts had become so large that Esther did not want them touched; her hair grew coarse; she sat before a mirror, watching for other changes. And now, she dreamed about Phillip nightly, she suffered between her sheets, but it was the truth; she had not wanted him born.

Esther the White had worried that a child of hers might be marked. He might appear with a rose at his tiny shoulder, with a butterfly on his forehead, a cross beneath one knee. She did not know if Mischa was the father; but she suspected that the tattooed man, Solo, had left something growing inside, something to remind her that she had once felt something, that she had once been in love. She cried slow tears as she sat in the porcelain tub which rested upon four lion's claws, and she imagined that her womb was filling with rising steam. Often, in her dreams, Esther the White saw her body turning a ghostly white, her skin becoming soft as apricots, the ends of her long pale hair turning a faint, watery green.

They lived then in a section of Notting Hill, and it was on the Bayswater Road that Mischa saw the hand-painted sign in a heavy leaded-glass window of a rooming house. Inge advertised herself as a bilingual nanny, nurse, housemaid, babysitter, and cook. When Mischa interviewed her, in the dark brown sitting room of the boarding house, Inge wore a black dress spotted with blue and yellow flowers. She wore the same dress when she aided in Phillip's birth, that day when Esther the White refused midwives, doctors, and hospitals, in the hope that the delivery in the parlor of their flat might give her a better chance, and Phillip a worse one.

Esther the White refused to look at the child. For the first week of Phillip's life she breast-fed him in the dark—at night, or in an unlit room. Slowly, she began to examine him. She touched his stomach and his arms while he gurgled or cried. She searched for markings—raised skin, strange colors, pigmentations. But he appeared to be unmarked. His eyes were brown, like Mischa's, his skin was as white as Esther's own. When he cried in his crib, and his gums changed from pale pink to red, Esther thought he looked like a howling rabbit.

Esther the White did not go to America. "Travel with an infant?" Mischa had said. "Let's wait till he gets a little bigger. Pneumonia is easy to catch on a ship. Wait." And Esther waited, but Phillip was catching mumps and flu, but Phillip was growing up, and Mischa's business was doing well. The child might have been a punishment for her affair with the tattooed man, so Esther the White did not complain; she continued to wait, until London became as familiar to her as the village of her childhood, until New York was a place she no longer mentioned, until she nearly forgot the jade pendant which could buy her passage on an ocean liner.

Inge, the nursemaid, did not believe Phillip was either adorable or horrid. He was a child. She had held dozens of them. What they needed was discipline and structure and a smack on the head. Phillip's crib was at the foot of Inge's bed; and he seemed to cry each time she invited a lover into that bed. But that was not extraordinary, and Inge would quickly rise from the bed and smack Phillip's hands; then his cries would turn to small hiccups as he forced himself to be silent. By the time Phillip spoke his first word ("No"—not at all an unusual first word), Mischa and Inge had become lovers.

Esther the White had decided that she wanted a life separate from Mischa's. She did not take lovers, for she was afraid that her body might again be claimed by some child growing inside. But she did have men. "Go ahead," Mischa would tell her, "go off with your boyfriends." He would sit and sulk in the parlor until Esther the White returned from her meetings at restaurants or parks or cinemas. Yet, Esther did choose her friends with the thought of bettering the family's situation. Often, they were men of property—building inspectors, contractors, or landlords. Men who were blue-eyed and pale-skinned, and who could help Mischa obtain a mortgage, or wire a flat that had faulty electricity, or find a cheap piece of property in the East End. Often these men were handsome, more often they were not. But all of them believed that Esther the White was beautiful; so beautiful that to be seen with her pale hand hanging onto their arms at the theater or at parties where sherry and scotch and cucumber sandwiches were served was well worth the price of making Mischa rich.

Still, Esther the White was not happy. She knew of Mischa's affair with Inge, and she was relieved by it. She cared a great deal for Mischa: she arranged her own affairs to his profit, she stroked his hand in darkened rooms when he was depressed about business, but she wished to sleep alone; the thought of making love chilled her, turned her eyes cold with the fear of pregnancy. When her spells of melancholy grew into sorrow, Esther the White decided that London itself was causing her unhappiness.

She came to despise anything British. Little Phillip had begun to speak, and when Esther discovered that his accent was English, she pounded a fist on an oak table top.

"Make him stop talking that way," she shouted at Inge. "I won't allow him to sound British."

When Phillip addressed Esther as "Mummy," Esther threatened to fire Inge, convinced that the nursemaid had taught her son to speak in a manner which would infuriate her.

Luckily, Mischa's business was prospering, for Esther

would no longer speak to British businessmen, let alone dine with them. Now the men she went out with were all foreigners: an Indian with whom she visited museums, a French Jew who read his poetry to her and tried to convince her to rejoin the religious tribe she had rejected. Yet throughout her sadness and her dissatisfaction with England, Esther continued to kiss Phillip goodnight, to watch for peculiarities, and to have as near to nothing to do with him as possible. He was not particularly handsome, but that was no crime. All in all, Esther was satisfied with Phillip as a child. However, when Phillip was six and began primary school, Mischa discovered that Inge's disciplinary methods included holding the child's head in a brimming sinkful of water. Mischa was horrified that the woman who cooed sweet German words to him while making love was holding his terrified son's head under water for any minor infraction of discipline.

"Pig," he said to her. "Are you crazy? Am I paying a madwoman to torture my son?"

Inge's eyes were wide. "What is so unusual?" she said, her hands dripping water onto the tile floor. "This is the way to discipline children. And he is a child, no?"

"God in heaven," Mischa moaned, "is this payment for my sins?" He knew that some punishment for his adultery would fall, and now it had. He waved a finger at Inge. "Lunatic," he screamed. But while Mischa was raging, Phillip held close to Inge's skirt. His head dripped with water, pools formed in his eyes. And, silently, he prayed that they would not take him away from the woman who loved him, the one who held him close.

"We have to fire Inge," Mischa told Esther.

Esther tossed her long hair. "No, we need her."

Mischa did not want to discuss the incident at the sink; why shouldn't Esther be protected? He shook his head. "What do we need her for?"

Esther was panicky; she knew nothing about children. She

especially wanted nothing to do with Phillip, who might betray her at any moment by sprouting a tattoo across his thin shoulders. "I don't even know how to change a diaper," she said.

"Esther," Mischa sighed, "he's six years old. He doesn't wear diapers."

"How can I live without Inge?" Esther insisted, though she hadn't spoken more than ten sentences to Inge in the past year. Who would take care of Phillip? To whose bed would Mischa creep at midnight? "Oh, no. I can't live without her," Esther cried.

"But she's a crazy woman," Mischa said. "She punishes our son by torturing him. She dips his head in water until he's blue. She is fired," he said. "She must go, today."

Esther the White held a hand to her forehead. A flicker of grief passed through her, as if Phillip had drowned in that sink Mischa spoke of. She wondered what her reaction might have been if Phillip had died as the nursemaid held his head under water, in the quiet bathroom. What had happened, Esther quickly decided, was as much her own fault as if she had held Phillip's head down herself. She must never have anything to do with children.

"All right," Esther said. She stared into her husband's eyes, to the yellow lines which spun out from the center of his irises. "All right. Fire her. We should never have hired her in the first place, with no references. But don't expect anything of me. He is your responsibility."

Mischa did not expect anything of Esther the White for more than ten years. Still, several times a year Esther would feel the weight of some enormous sadness, but then the sadness would pass, and it was as easily forgotten as the jade pendant that was hidden in the lining of an old fox coat. Mischa did not expect anything at all from Esther the White until Phillip started walking into the water. After the first occurrence in the Serpentine, Esther the White decided Phillip was suicidal; she told Mischa to let the boy be—suicidal adolescence would pass, and Mischa could not convince her the situation was serious. But by the third summer, when Phillip was nearly twenty and he had already tried to drown himself three times, the last time wearing Mischa's own hound's-tooth sport jacket, Mischa expected something of Esther.

"You have to do something," Mischa said. He was particularly infuriated that his sport jacket had been ruined in the Thames.

"There's nothing to do. It's obvious that he wants to kill himself."

"Is that a mother? Is that the voice of a mother?" Mischa said.

Esther the White shrugged. Personally, she had never thought of herself as a mother. "You asked, I told," she said.

Recently, Esther the White had acquired a new boyfriend, but this one was a lover as well. He, too, was a foreigner—from Brooklyn, New York. His name was Shapiro, and he inspired in Esther both passion for sex and a fresh desire for New York. Shapiro had left a bad marriage; he now drove a taxi in London, and the two would often drive together for hours, Shapiro murmuring the praises of Brooklyn, and the American way, American women who walked down Fifth Avenue like they owned the world. He was ten years younger than Esther, but with him, Shapiro promised, it would be impossible to conceive. Hence, his bad marriage to a wife who wanted at least three children, and Esther the White's passion. Often, she would go with him, up to his room near Paddington. There they made love; the taxi driver would whisper in his thick foreign New York accent, and Esther would stare at objects around the room—a hairbrush, a vest, a blue airmail letter, and she would imagine that each had traveled the distance from New York.

She was not particularly interested in Phillip at this point: she had a lover, she had the desire to leave a country she was bound to by her family; plus she had never wanted him born.

Phillip was not in the room, so Esther the White was perfectly frank.

"Sorry," she shrugged. "I know nothing about children."

At that time, Phillip was seated on a maroon velvet couch in the study. He shook his head. He dripped water. He eavesdropped and agreed with his mother—his parents should leave him alone. However, Phillip had not wanted to kill himself, and he truly felt sorry about ruining the hound's-tooth jacket. He wanted only to be left alone. Alone, so that he could merge with the water. He believed any water was beautiful, whether for its dark waves or for its slow-moving currents. He wanted to be a part of that beauty, traveling at a natural speed through the waves, without effort.

"I'm not saying Phillip's right," Esther continued. "Maybe he's crazy. But if he wants to do something crazy, who does it hurt? Maybe himself, but that's his right."

Phillip, the eavesdropper, nodded solemnly and agreed.

"Me," Mischa declared. "His father. It hurts me. It hurts the floor, it hurts my jacket, it hurts my reputation, it's an insult to me as his father."

Esther the White reconsidered. She thought of her lover, Shapiro, and the wonderful Brooklyn that was now living inside of her soul. She pursed her mouth and breathed heavily. "Take him to America," she said.

"For what?" Mischa asked. His business was booming with semidetached houses, why go to America?

"You'll see," Esther the White smiled. "The move will cure him. Take him to America."

"What?" Mischa said. "I thought you were over that. He doesn't need America, he needs a wife."

"A wife?" Esther said. "What would he do with a wife?"

"Phillip, in here," Mischa called. "Get in here."

Phillip was standing in the doorway before Mischa called his name.

"Yes?" Phillip said.

"Yes?" Mischa mimicked. Esther the White quickly slipped on the dark glasses she had taken to wearing whenever she drove through the city in Shapiro's taxi. "Not yes," Mischa said. "No. I've had enough of this walking into water. Enough."

Phillip stubbed out his cigarette in a small egg-shaped ashtray; he hung his head like a hound.

"Let me ask you this." Mischa sat heavily in a cushioned chair and bit off the tip of a cigar. "How long have you had this . . . urge?"

"Father, I'm really interested in water from a philosophical point of view. I just get carried away."

"I ask why you're embarrassing me, why you're killing yourself, and you tell me about philosophy?"

"It's not that I want to hurt myself. It's just that the water seems so purifying, so much cleaner."

"Cleaner?" Mischa bellowed. "Cleaner than what?" He turned to Esther the White and whispered: "We have a lunatic for a son, we have a lunatic."

"We'll take him to America," Esther the White whispered in answer to her husband.

"What did I do? Did I do something wrong?" Mischa said.

"Not at all," Phillip said, not daring to say that he had been imagining diving deep into the water for years. In primary school he had practiced holding his breath under water, so that he could stare up to watch the way the light filtered through the top of the water during swim practice. And when he finished school, at seventeen, Phillip had begun to dream of rivers and seas. In a notebook he drew the plants and the fish that swam through his dreams. Once there was a gray porpoise, which he followed for some time. Another night, he found a flower which seemed to be a sea rose, tiny and white. But he had also attended parties, he took girls out on dates to the cinema, he had many friends and began to work for his father. He had seemed, to Mischa and Esther the White, absolutely unmarked. Yet he was happiest dreaming, or drawing his visions into his leather-bound notebook.

"Why, you haven't done anything at all to me," Phillip told his parents. "I walk close to the water, and then suddenly, before I know it, I'm in some river or pool."

"We're getting you married, then we'll see how far you walk," Mischa told his son.

"But I don't know anyone I'd want to marry," Phillip said.

Mischa laughed. "Want. Did you hear him, Esther? Want."

"I heard him," Esther said. "I still say, leave him alone, forget the wife, and let's go to New York."

But Mischa was convinced he was right. He was convinced that Phillip only needed "settling" like a foundation. Yet when Phillip was persuaded to date the daughter of an acquaintance of Mischa's, an Anglican girl who studied art, he drove to the Thames and jumped in. The art student telephoned from the hospital, where Phillip had been taken, and where the water was now being pumped from his lungs. "We were having such a good time," the girl told Esther the White, "until he saw the water."

On the other end of the wire, Esther the White smiled. She held a linen handkerchief over the receiver and turned to Mischa; and he stared back into the pale eyes he had always feared as a child, eyes he sometimes forgot belonged to his wife.

"We'll take him to America," she whispered, not because she thought Phillip could be cured in New York, but because she ached for America, she longed for it, and had planned, when she had first stepped outside the ice of her childhood village, to get there, no matter what it took.

Mischa nodded in agreement and defeat, and he stared at her in silence as Esther the White hung up the phone. Esther the White smiled lightly, that afternoon, when Phillip rested in a hospital bed, but her heart was pounding, her fingers twitched. "We're almost there," she whispered, to no one in particular. "Almost."

But now, safe in America, resting between cool sheets, in an ebony bed, Esther the White still felt she hadn't arrived, she was still only almost there. It was an American sky outside her window, but she could not sleep; it was New York air out there, still she dreamed of Phillip. And she seemed suddenly to have lost all of her courage; she was afraid.

She, who as a girl could have faced anything, even the wild ice that surrounded the village where she was born, was now terrified of a quiet death between soft feathered pillows. What she had set out to do long ago had been accomplished—she had left the past behind and come to New York; but there was no white-maned lion inside her now; there was only air, cold quivering air. And because the night simply would not go away, Esther the White sat at her window and wondered how, at this late date, she could change her life; how she might, finally, ride the night to sleep.

2

They had locked Phillip in the smallest of the cottages. And although Esther the White dreamed each night that her son was drowning, the padlock on the pink wooden door was unnecessary; Phillip was exhausted. An oar from the rescue boat had placed a gash in his scalp; and had the family unlocked his door, the sunlight might have done Phillip some good, for his lungs were tired and blue.

Lisa brought him plum jam, tea, and kasha with noodles. Max spent an entire afternoon playing poker with his nephew, until he noticed that Phillip was busy stuffing cards up his sleeve. Mischa did not believe in pampering the ill; and both Esther the White and Esther the Black avoided the cottage—

they could not bear to see Phillip this way. On the seventh day of his recovery, Rose walked down the overgrown path to Phillip's door.

"Whatever did I do to deserve such a hot day as this one," Rose groaned as she locked the door behind her and slipped the key into her pocket. She walked through the darkened room and began opening curtains. Phillip sat on a wooden rocker, turning pages of a *National Geographic* which a local physician had brought to the cottage several summers before when Phillip's drowning had led to complications: a severe ear infection and partial deafness. Phillip smoked a cigarette and leafed through a picture essay on Montreal.

"I said," Rose repeated, hands on her hips, "whatever did I do to deserve it?"

"Meaning the burden I am?" Phillip smiled.

"Of course not," Rose said. "Darling," she called him, and then she waved a hand through the unmoving air. "The heat," she said. "Never you."

"Article on new frontiers in the West, in this issue," Phillip said of the *National Geographic.*

"Really?" Rose moved closer.

Phillip nodded. "Arizona."

Rose refused the magazine. "I'm only interested in Nevada. You should know that by now."

They were silent, until Phillip said, "I'm feeling quite well today."

"Wonderful," Rose said, but she was distracted. She kicked off her thin-strapped purple sandals. "Fine, but I'm worried about Esther."

"Our Esther?" Phillip fanned himself with his magazine. "Don't you think it's a bit warmer in here now that you've opened the curtains and let the sun in?"

"Truth is," Rose frowned, "I think something's wrong with her."

"Our Esther?" Phillip said, as he offered Rose a mint.

"Truth is," Rose lowered her voice, "I think she's planning to screw us all. That's what I think."

Phillip slowly chewed a green mint; he thought about his daughter and then reached for another mint.

"Phillip, did you hear me?"

"Dear, what would you like me to do? I'm an invalid." He handled the folds of his blue bathrobe and smiled.

Rose sighed. "Do you have anything to drink in here?"

She herself had stocked the cottage with bottles of tequila and gin.

"Cabinet," Phillip said.

"And naturally no ice," Rose said. "I'll have to settle for straight gin." She poured some into a glass and sat down across from Phillip, in a large loveseat. She crossed her bare feet and sipped her drink. "I don't know what will happen next. A heat wave. Trouble with Esther the Black. A hurricane."

Phillip shrugged and continued to eat mints. Both of them knew that nothing ever happened at the Compound, except for Phillip's own drownings. They sat together like two old friends, in silence. Rose settled back into her flowered cushion.

"Any chance of your finding a way to get to Nevada?" Phillip asked.

"Not one chance." Rose smiled.

"Tell me," Phillip asked. "What is it about that place that attracts you so?" A state without water, a state with no escape.

"The climate is so nice and hot in Nevada," Rose answered.

"But, dear," Phillip said, "you hate the heat."

"Yes, but it's clean there. A clean sort of heat."

"When will you ever scrape the money together?" Phillip sighed.

Rose shrugged. "Perhaps when you die—there's your insurance, and your parents will just have to help support me."

"Awfully sorry," Phillip apologized.

"But Esther the Black," Rose said. "She could ruin everything. She could make your mother so angry that you'll be sent upstate to a psycho ward, and I'll be on the streets. After all these years."

"Rose," Phillip warned.

"Well, it's true," Rose said. "She's a troublemaker. I've seen her leaving the house early in the morning. God knows what she's up to. She probably has a lover in town. Or maybe one of the fishermen." Rose snorted. "Something has to be done."

"I'm telling you right now, Rose," Phillip said, and Rose stared up at him as if it were a rational man who spoke. "Leave the girl alone. You have to forget about running her life. How you could have arranged a marriage for her in the first place, so many years ago, is beyond me. People just don't do that anymore. Not even for an inheritance."

"Oh, what do you know about what people do?" Rose pouted.

"I read a lot," Phillip snapped, but both of them knew all he ever read were back issues of *National Geographic.* Phillip lashed out at Rose because he was tired; he was always tired after a drowning. Still, he cared for Rose and was sorry to disappoint her. She was the girl's mother, and she wanted for Esther the Black what her own mother in Bridgeport had wanted for her. A husband, a lovely quiet life. And money. Enough money for all of them. Phillip lit a cigarette and then asked brightly, "What's it like out? Low tide?"

Rose poured herself another glass of gin. Really she thought, Phillip was gracious, understanding. He would have gladly sent her off to Las Vegas. If the credit cards had been in Phillip's name, rather than in his father's, Rose might have been, at that very moment, drinking a cold gin and tonic beside the pool at the Dunes Hotel. He knew nothing about children, of course; he knew nothing of the fear Rose knew each time he attempted suicide and Rose had to face the possibility of expulsion from the Compound.

"Yes," Rose answered. "It's low tide." She did not really know if it was or not, she hadn't bothered to glance at the beach as she walked down the path to Phillip's cottage, but she did not want to take the image of low tide away from her husband; those slick stones, as they appeared when the salt water first rolled away and left green algae and seaweed stranded on the beach, made Phillip smile. Rose finished her drink, she avoided the topic of Esther the Black; after all, Phillip was a sick man. So, she spoke of the boredom of spending an afternoon in St. Fredrics, she told Phillip what was served for dinner all week, she described a troupe of sixteen bluejays that had taken up residence in the mimosa trees outside Esther the White's bedroom window. Phillip listened, and he rocked back and forth in his chair; and then he walked to the window and lifted the heavy curtain in his hand. He was so tired that he might no longer have the strength to scale the sea wall; he wondered if Cohen would still manage to follow him.

The cottage had been chosen for Phillip's recoveries because it was the only house in the Compound without a water view. But Phillip still struggled to see the harbor, although he could see only the beginnings of the eastern section of the Compound, where there were no flowers, only weeds—honeysuckle and orange wood lilies—and where the pine grove towered above the sea wall. And there, standing in front of the grove, was Phillip's daughter. For years Phillip had lied to himself; he told himself he had been given the name for his daughter in a dream he had the night after the girl was born. But, in fact, he knew what his mother's reaction would be; he knew that when Esther the Black's name was written permanently, in ink, on the birth certificate, Esther the White would shudder. He knew that even though Esther the White had given up all things of the past, even her surname, she still believed in ghosts, and he wanted, more than anything else, to haunt his mother, even after he himself was dead.

And now he watched: Esther the Black walked across the

lawn; she was readying herself for a meeting with Ira Rath. She wore jeans and a red-and-black striped T-shirt, and when she finally stopped pacing on the wide green lawn, she stared in the direction of Phillip's window. Her dark hair hid her face, and Phillip could not see her eyes, but he knew where she stared. He thought how cruel it had been for him and Rose to have both used the girl in their fights against Esther the White. And he wondered if Esther the Black was haunting not only her grandmother but Phillip as well. They watched each other for some time, they stared across the yards as Rose continued to speak of the bluejays outside Esther the White's window, who were so tame they were not afraid to snatch crusts of white bread from the palm of the old woman's hand.

Esther the Black stood with her hands on her hips. She could see only Phillip's shadow, or the movement of the curtain as it swayed behind the glass. For a moment she imagined that there was nothing she could not do; if she wanted, she could speak to him, across the lawn, through the glass, the locked door, the hard wood. Even though they rarely talked, she now imagined that she could reach him. But, instead she turned, quite suddenly, as if she had heard something call from beyond the pine grove. There was no use standing and staring; she had to meet Ira Rath, she had to make her plans. So, Esther the Black turned and left Phillip alone at his window. And he was still watching as she began to walk over the pine needles, feeling them crush beneath her sandals as they sent out their fragrance into the full air.

Esther the Black walked out of Phillip's sight; believing that her father wanted to be saved, when he only wanted not to be haunted. And she walked as quickly as she could to St. Fredrics, where she would meet Ira Rath.

When she walked into the Starfish Lounge, Ira Rath was already there, sitting at a rear table, drinking dark beer. Esther had not seen him since he had first gone off to college, and Ira had changed, he had let his hair grow wild, and his bluejeans were faded and tight; a safety pin hung from his earlobe, dangling nearly to his collar.

"Ira?" Esther the Black said, wondering if she had mistaken someone else for the accountant's son.

Ira Rath rose. "Esther," he said, taking her hand. "What took you? I've been waiting for twenty minutes, and the place you chose for our rendezvous is a dump."

They sat together and ordered beer. Esther the Black examined him. "You look different," she said.

"I am different. I'm totally into my music. I'm about to move into a loft apartment with my band, The Quick and the Mad. I've even legally changed my name, but I haven't told my father yet; too much of a shock."

Esther the Black narrowed her eyes; if Ira Rath had been a stranger, if she hadn't remembered Friday-night dinners where Ira, dressed in a blue suit, had sat between Solomon Rath and Esther the White, spooning up his second helping of pudding, Esther the Black might have found him attractive. "What is your name now?" she asked.

"Pagan. Pagan Rath." He swallowed beer. "It's a name that's more consistent with the style of music I play."

Esther the Black wrinkled her brow; the family would never approve of marriage to someone with a name like Pagan. "We won't mention your name change to my family," she said.

"Punk," Pagan Rath said to Esther. "That's my sound. Punk Rock."

"Well, never mind," Esther said. "Music is music."

"I've got a song," Pagan Rath said. "Once my song catches on, I'll have it made. That's why I'm willing to consider tricking your family out of some of their money. 'Nova Scotia Avenue' is the name of my tune," he smiled. "Remember that title; it'll be at the top of the charts."

Esther smiled tightly. She did not own a radio, and she had difficulty sympathizing with the Ira she had always known as a rock musician. He had grown up in a brownstone, he had A.T.&T. stocks in his name.

"What about your stocks?" Esther asked.

"Sold," Pagan told her. "To buy leather outfits for The Quick and the Mad and a skunk-fur coat for myself."

"Well, we're both broke," Esther the Black said. "But I have a plan that we could both profit from."

Pagan's eyes were closed; quite suddenly he began to pound his palms on the table top in a simulated drum roll. He sang the opening bars of "Nova Scotia Avenue":

"There's ice on the streetcorners / and tears on your face / but don't worry baby / I'll soon win that race."

"Ira," Esther the Black interrupted, "this is my plan. We work together. We announce that we plan to marry right away. My grandparents should be good for at least a thousand dollars for the wedding dress, the trousseau, the rabbi's fees. Only none of their money will ever get to the bridal shop or the rabbi—we'll split it, you and me. Eighty percent for me, twenty for you."

"Fifty-fifty," Pagan Rath said.

"Ira, please," Esther sighed. "Don't be difficult."

"The name is Pagan," he corrected. "And the ruse isn't worth it for twenty percent. Maybe I can raise the cash to cut a record, but I still have to hire a promoter, an agent, a couple of roadies. And I don't have time to fool around, Esther, because one thing I know for sure: I'm slated for immortality, and your grandparents' cash can help me out. You're my oldest friend, kid," Pagan shrugged, "but when destiny calls, then it's business. Then it's fifty percent."

It was nearly dinnertime, and Esther the Black and Ira Rath were expected at the main house. Esther did not have much of a choice; without Ira, she was without a plan. So she agreed to the bargain the accountant's son offered, and she called a taxi to pick them up at the Starfish Lounge. In the taxi,

Esther the Black persuaded Pagan to comb his hair and remove his safety pin and worn aviator's jacket. These, Esther assured him, would be quite safe under the rhododendron bush near the Compound gate.

As they got out of the taxi and walked toward the gate, Pagan Rath spoke of his musician's life; he boasted of oral sex and cocaine and put his arm around Esther. "Listen," he said, "maybe we can get it on after dinner."

Esther the Black frowned. "What are you talking about?"

"You know," Pagan smiled. "Love."

"Oh, Ira," Esther said, as she leaned her head on the window, "this is business. Don't be ridiculous."

Pagan Rath threw up his hands. "All right," he said. "But some day you'll beg me for some loving, and you won't be the first."

Esther the Black paid the taxi driver, and she watched as Pagan hid his punk clothes in the bushes. Now that it was nearly time to put her plan into action, Esther was afraid. She wondered exactly where she would go once she had rescued her parents from the Compound, once she was free. And as Esther the Black walked up the path which led to her grandparents' house, she tried to convince herself that all her fears were unfounded; she had walked up the same path thousands of times before, she had eaten at their table every night of her life, and her plan to deceive them was foolproof; before she knew it she would walk out of the Compound gate for the last time. There was really nothing to be afraid of. All the same, when they walked up the stairs to the wide wooden porch, Esther the Black swallowed hard; and she was not practicing any sort of deception when she asked Pagan if she could hold his hand.

3

That evening, as Esther the White began the Friday-night meal, as she prepared the salmon with lemon juice, scallions, and parsley, she looked out the kitchen window and saw Mischa speaking with his brother, the dwarf. Mischa's arm reached down to encircle Max's shoulders, and the dwarf spoke with a great many furious gestures. And as Esther the White slipped the salmon into the oven, as she began the cold, uncooked lemon mousse, cutting lemons at the sink and pouring the cream into a brown wooden bowl, her face grew pale. She looked out of the window again.

Out there, where the honeysuckle was as thick as the air, Max was waving his hand, pointing to the sea wall and the large, green lawn. Esther the White held the empty cream carton in her hand: she strained to look out the window; she wished that she could read lips, but she could only stare from her window, and worry. She did not trust the dwarf; he was her enemy, who, for years, had been trying to convince Mischa to sell the Compound, the land that Esther the White had always dreamed of, even before the night she left her old village. Before, in other years, she might have been certain that Mischa would not listen to his brother, but now their finances were poor, and no one knew that better than Esther the White, who kept close tabs on the accountant, Rath. So, now Mischa might listen. Now, in the honeysuckle air, he might lean close to his brother's mouth; and Esther the White had never trusted Max, she never regretted leaving him with the circus.

For his part, Max had not pined long for Mischa and Esther the White. In his first year with the circus he traveled to Spain, to Finland, to Denmark and Holland. He had enjoyed the circus exhibition, where he stood on a detachable wooden platform alongside the circus manager, Solo, the tattooed man, and Thea, a woman from Munich, who sang like an angel and was covered with hair like a bear.

Max asked that the greyhounds be fed larger portions of meat each week, so that they would not be quite as vicious. He had many ideas for the circus, which Solo put forth to the owner, Jules, as his own. Max began to attend the cinema in every city the circus visited, and he particularly loved the films of Fred Astaire. He elaborated on the steps he had learned from Madame Laverne in Marseilles, and taught himself to tap dance; soon he became one of the largest attractions in the circus. In under a year, Max had completely forgotten what Esther the White looked like; he hadn't cared much for her anyway.

Quickly, Max taught himself bookkeeping, and he became invaluable to Solo, the manager, who never paid close attention to the books he was supposed to keep, as he preferred to spend his days in a cloud of opium. The crowds loved Max and his bold tap dancing to new American tunes. Thea from Munich let him snuggle close whenever the circus traveled from one city to another by train; so he was almost never lonely, and, if he ever was, Max would find his way to the sea turtle's cage. Here he would lie in the sweet-smelling sawdust, bringing carrots and grains as gifts. He whispered and sang, and rested beneath the fin of the huge turtle he named Miriam. Protected by Miriam's leathery green arm, beneath her gray veins, Max was comfortable, at ease. He would stroke her shell back, and speak of his sexual longings, and he would whisper about his jealousy of Solo, who worked the dwarf without praise or recognition, and who never had a kind word for anyone except for the ladies, who fell in love with him quick as a sigh.

In time, the circus owner, Jules, discovered that Solo was the cause of his financial woes. The tattooed man had been slipping a third of the circus profits into his own pocket; he needed money, gold, and jewels to buy opium and to impress the women who followed him into bed in every city he visited. Max was stunned when he heard of Solo's treachery; the manager had been a hero of sorts, for Max's imagination had been fired by the stories Solo told of breasts and thighs. Solo claimed to have sired two dozen children, and he was certain there were more, that he had left his mark in Germany and France.

And so, when Jules discovered Solo to be a thief, and the tattooed man disappeared in the south of Spain, with several thousand dollars of the circus money and a pair of silver salt shakers which had belonged to Jules's mother, Max was convinced that the circus would disband, and he would be left without a career, without a home. But his despair lifted when Jules asked him to become the circus manager. The financial troubles diminished, and the troupe acquired a small, but glowing reputation. After some years, Max became a partner; Jules wondered what he had ever done without the dwarf, and he blessed the day Solo disappeared.

And so, Max had little time for tap dancing; he was concerned with business matters now. To replace his own act, he bought, from a grieving couple in Hungary, their tiny daughter, Jenna, whom Max taught to dance. Yet Max remained a man of solitude; he spent hours in Miriam's cage; after a day at work on the financial receipts, he would hurry there to smoke cigars, and stare at the sky. He had plenty of candy—chocolate cherries and sweet molasses babies. His small suits were made of linen, silk, and fine wool. The entire troupe respected him; Jules called him sonny. Still, he was unhappy.

His real worry, at that time of his life, when he had been with the circus for nearly fifteen years, was that he had never had a woman. He missed Solo's stories of love and of passion; he feared he would live his whole life without feeling his blood pulse. He began to walk through the circus crowds, searching for someone to fall in love with.

Jules shook his head. "That's not the way to do it," the circus owner told his small partner. "You'll never find a woman that way."

But, outside Vienna, where the circus had set up cages and tents on a large circular village green, Max saw Lisa. He fell, instantly and with no trouble at all, in love.

Lisa was years younger than Max; she was just twenty-five. Her legs were long, the legs of a dancer. When Max finally approached her, after hours of soul searching on the floor of the sea turtle's cage, the top of his head reached Lisa's waist. He asked if she were a dancer, and Lisa was stunned; that was exactly what she wished to be. Max pulled no punches, he wasted no time; immediately, he admitted that he believed Lisa was the most beautiful woman he had ever seen. True, he was a dwarf, but he had traveled all over the continent and he had learned his smile from the tattooed man. Lisa was flattered. They dined, that night, on veal, calves' liver and onions. Later in the week he sent her violets and opals. On the day the troupe was to leave the village, Max offered Lisa the chance to become a dancer with the circus. She accepted. Some months later, in a town in Bavaria—which particularly depressed Max, for it vaguely reminded him of his own childhood village—the two were married.

Max lost all signs of depression. He rarely visited the sea turtle's cage, and when he did it was only to lie in the sawdust and sing Lisa's praises. He spoke so often of how Lisa's eyes were like two black berries that the sea turtle rolled away in boredom and disgust. Max could not have been happier. Lisa, however, was crushed when Jules decided that her dancing was inappropriate for the circus.

"She tries to dance beautifully," Jules whispered to Max. "If they want to see beautiful, they don't come here. That's not what they come to the circus to see."

To cheer Lisa, Max and Jules devised a plan for an American tour. Each night, before Max made love to Lisa, he would repeat the names of American cities which Jules had decided to include in their tour.

"Minneapolis," he would whisper to her as he slowly kissed her knees, both thighs. "Pittsburgh, Philadelphia, Trenton, New Jersey."

The American tour was neither a success nor a failure. One of the greyhounds froze in its cage as the troupe crossed the Atlantic; but the minute the ship docked in Boston, Jules hired a Yugoslavian shipman who was a juggler, and so all losses were covered. Lisa began to cheer up: she loved traveling on the super highways in the troupe's yellow truck; when they reached Miami she pinched Max's nose, kissed him, and sighed. Miami was paradise to Lisa, but the circus could not stay, they had barely scratched America's surface. The surprising thing about the tour was its length. After several years, it seemed they hadn't covered a third of the country. So they kept on, playing American towns and cities, finishing up the Southeast and the Midwest. At the beginning of the northeastern route, Max began to read newspapers, hoping to polish up his

English so that he would no longer embarrass Lisa in restaurants. On a Thursday, in a truck traveling through New Jersey, Max was reading an issue of *The New York Times* which the fat lady had lent him. A small article in the real-estate section described the Compound; and there in black and white, in English, was the name the brothers had allowed Esther the White to choose for them in the stable at Marseilles.

"My brother must be a millionaire. It says he has his own housing development. He *is* a millionaire," Max whispered hotly to Lisa as the circus traveled down the New Jersey Turnpike, in search of a campground.

The two began to whisper conspiratorially, although the only one who might have heard them was the Yugoslavian juggler.

"This is America?" the juggling sailor asked, in Yugoslavian, a language no one in the troupe understood.

When they pitched their tents in southern Jersey, Jules cried out, "What's here? Swamps? Quicksand?"

Max approached his partner. "I'm getting out, my friend. I'm leaving the business."

"Look," Jules tried to pacify the dwarf. "We won't be in New Jersey for more than another week. It's not that bad; you can take it."

"No, no. It's not New Jersey that's getting to me. I found out I got a brother here." Jules shrugged. "A rich one," Max continued. "And I'm staying in America."

Lisa encouraged Max to quit the business. And, when she heard of the cruel way in which Esther had sold Max, she cried out that Max should get every cent, every piece of linen, silverware, and jewelry that he could from his brother. And, really, she was disappointed in circus life, and felt that she and Max could do much better, now that they had seen the wealth that flowed in America. Jules handed over half of all the partners had saved; and the two shook hands solemnly. The dwarf walked by the sea turtle's cage one last time; there were tears in his eyes, but since his marriage their relationship had become nothing, mere memory—and the sea turtle barely blinked an old yellow eye when the taxi came to a stop in front of her cage, and collected Max and his wife.

Max was not overflowing with family feeling, of his childhood he remembered little; but his feet had begun to ache from the years of dancing, and from the constant traveling, and he knew Lisa was unhappy.

When the taxi pulled up in front of the porch of the main house, the family was drinking tea. Esther the Black was days old; her cradle rocked of its own accord, with the air. When Esther the White saw the small figure of a man in the cab, she felt faint. She walked to Mischa and placed a hand on his arm.

"Company?" Rose asked.

"No," Esther said. "Not company."

What seemed to Rose and Phillip to be a child of ten stood on the dirt road. Behind followed a tall, blond woman, carrying an enormous leather pocketbook. The taxi driver began to unload suitcases and trunks.

"What do you know!" Phillip said happily. "That's not a child, he's a dwarf."

As Max climbed up the porch steps with great difficulty, Esther the Black began to wail in her cradle. The dwarf did not look very much different, so perhaps Mischa was only dreaming that his brother, the Baby, was walking up the stairs of his house, dressed in a three-piece sky-blue suit. For Mischa had dreamed of his brother for a quarter of a century. It had been the Baby who appeared to Mischa each night, faithfully, and advised Mischa in matters of business and matters of the heart. At times, most often at three or four in the morning, Max would appear at the foot of Mischa's bed, covered by a small imaginary quilt, and knowingly he would call Mischa a dog, a traitor, a flea. Mischa blinked his large brown and yellow eyes; for here the brother of his dreams stood before him. He was speechless. But Esther the White was not. She was furious that

Max had found them; she had helped the dwarf escape from their childhood village, she had found a career for him, and, in return, she expected him to leave her and Mischa alone, free of the past.

"Just what do you think you're doing here?" she said to Max as he peered into Esther the Black's cradle.

Max chuckled; he bent over the crying child and stroked her small forehead. Max then walked to Mischa, stretched out his small hand, and said: "Let's let bygones be bygones."

Mischa was speechless, but he nodded his agreement, and embraced the dwarf with such power that he lifted his brother into the air and spun him around.

Mischa and Max continued to embrace; Lisa dropped her heavy pocketbook on the porch with a thud; and Phillip ran off to the parlor for a bottle of sherry to celebrate his new uncle's arrival. Only Esther the White was silent; she sat heavily in her wicker chair, and she placed a hand on Esther the Black's cradle, and she rocked so hard that the wooden cradle nearly flew off the porch, carrying the child into the air. The dwarf's arrival was, Esther the White then believed, a bad omen: if the past could track her down so easily, anything might happen, the earth itself might move.

And now, as she watched the brothers, as the two stood in secrecy by the sea wall, Esther knew she had been right. No good was to come from a bond between her husband and Max. Esther the White shrugged. Let those two do as they want, she thought, as long as they don't involve me. As long as they leave me and my Compound alone. But she wondered if Max could forget that it was Esther who had sold him to the circus, and she wondered if Mischa could forget his guilt; and it seemed to her suddenly, as she poured lemons and cream and gelatin into a blender, that she was without power. Perhaps she had never really had any control over Mischa; perhaps she had always been alone.

She watched the brothers for a while longer, until she

could smell the salmon burning in the oven. And then she had to hurry to remove the pan before dinner was completely ruined. She burned her hand, though only very slightly; and when she poured cold water over her pale skin, no one would have noticed how her hands shook.

4

That evening, at dinner, just as Esther the White's lemon mousse was served, Mischa announced that he had decided to sell the eastern section of the Compound. Only the dinner guest, Ira "Pagan" Rath, continued to eat his dessert; everyone else grew silent.

"Frankly, I think you should sell the whole Compound," Max called out. "It was a lousy idea to begin with, and every one of us could use some cash."

"Of course," Mischa said to the family, "every idiot thinks he's an expert."

Lisa spooned sugar into Max's teacup, but the dwarf

pushed her arm away. "Did you just call me an idiot? Is that what I just heard?"

"My god," Esther the White said, so softly that she could barely be heard.

But Mischa ignored his wife; it was certainly easier to argue with his brother than to explain himself to Esther the White. He had never made an important decision without her before, and he would not have now, if the accountant, Solomon Rath, hadn't forced his hand. "Did he hear what I said, or is he deaf?" Mischa asked Lisa, as if she served as the dwarf's interpreter.

Esther the Black, who had planned this dinner so carefully around Ira Rath and who had expected to ask for her trousseau money that very evening, now realized that they had all forgotten that her fiancé was there. Pagan, himself, seemed oblivious to any commotion—he turned and asked Cohen if he could eat the landscape artist's dessert. Cohen's answer was an impatient wave of his arm; he was too busy watching Esther the White to waste time talking to the accountant's son.

In the center of the table stood a vase of white roses and tall, pale daisies. Max could not see over the vase. "Just a minute," he called out to his brother. "If you want a discussion with me, move the flowers." He raised his small voice. "Move the flowers."

"Esther," Rose said, and Esther the Black rose, lifted the flowers from the table, and placed the vase on the liquor cabinet.

"I like to see you when I talk," Max said. The brothers stared at each other. "So," Max said finally. "Tell me to my face that I don't have your best interests at heart. I agree with Solomon Rath—it's the right time to sell. In my opinion, if you let Rath sell everything now you would be smart."

Mischa had realized too late that he had lost control of the family's holdings. The decision to sell a large area of the Compound to Sam Gardner, the builder who had surrounded St. Fredrics with cheap housing developments, had been made by Solomon Rath. Rath had not even needed Mischa's signature on a piece of paper. As she sat at the table, pushing the untouched lemon mousse away from her, Esther the White did not have to be told that Mischa would never had made so huge a decision without her. She reached for a glass of water, but she could not swallow; all her life she had wanted a place that belonged to her, and she was about to lose a part of it, maybe the whole thing. There was no one to blame; she did not even bother to raise her eyes to Mischa. There was no one to blame but Esther the White herself—for she had been the one to help Solomon Rath gain power of attorney.

When Max arrived at the Compound, Esther the White was afraid. She imagined that the dwarf might ask for half of all their property—she imagined that Mischa might agree to make up for the years Max had traveled with the circus. And so, Esther the White had struck a bargain with Solomon Rath.

She had gone into Solomon Rath's office, as she always had; Mischa trusted her to take care of the family's finances, and since the failure of the Compound, he had no real heart for business anymore. The office was air-conditioned that day; ice formed on the window, even though Madison Avenue was steaming with heat. Esther the White quickly expressed her fear that Max might try to gain control of the family fortune, and she ignored the plate of rugulach Rath's secretary had set by her arm.

"Well," Rath had said, "we can't have that. No. We have to watch out for pikers and lost relatives." He reached for a piece of cake; crumbs stuck to the corners of his lips.

"My husband's naive," Esther the White said. "My husband's trusting. I know that everyone has to watch out for himself, and I want control of the property."

Rath tapped his forehead. "Smart," he said.

"But I don't want Mischa to get any funny ideas," Esther the White had said. "I wouldn't want him to think that I don't trust him."

"Of course," Rath had said. "What else is a marriage for?" He walked around his desk three times. And then he stopped, motionless on the beige Oriental rug. "Of course," he said. "What you need is an executor. Someone who knows the score—someone who's legally responsible for all business transactions and profits—but who knows whom to turn the profits over to—you."

"Yes." Esther the White smiled, and she accepted a styrofoam cup full of steamy dark tea from Rath. "Solomon Rath, you're just that person."

The necessary papers were drawn up that very afternoon. And when Esther the White returned to the Compound, she left the Cadillac's back seat so quickly that Cohen did not even have time to turn his head.

"Mischa," she said, when she walked in the front door. "Sign this." Esther the White handed him three copies of legal forms, and then sat on the velvet couch.

Mischa pulled a silver pen from his vest pocket. "Esther," he said, as he signed his name, "is this another of Rath's bad investments? Is this another chemical plant?"

"No," Esther the White had said, believing herself to be the perfect, careful wife. "It's insurance. Insurance against thieves."

But soon after, Esther the White discovered that Solomon Rath was not on her side; the accountant was watching out for himself.

"You have to understand," Rath told her at their next meeting, when Esther the White complained about a bounced check, "that I have to be very careful about the money you spend. I have investments to make. You and Mischa would be better off with a monthly allowance."

"What kind of investments?" Esther the White had asked.

"Esther," Solomon Rath sighed. "What do you know about business? Leave it to me."

"And what if I say no?" Esther the White asked.

Solomon Rath opened up his large palms and shrugged. "Then I'll have to insist," he had said.

But Esther the White had never thought Rath would sell the Compound; especially not to Gardner, a man who designed housing developments where every tree was uprooted; bulldozers would level every curve in the earth.

"Mother," Esther the Black called out, because she had no time to lose—the Compound was crumbling and she had to make her move if she wanted the cash she would need to make her escape. "Did you know that Ira is quite interested in music?"

Pagan Rath nodded as he spooned up his lemon mousse.

Rose had a lot to lose, and maybe something to gain, and her attention was focused on the brothers. "That's nice," she said absently to Esther the Black.

"If we're going to be honest with each other," Max said now, "the truth is that morally, and legally, I'm entitled to half of what the sale of the eastern section will bring."

"Here, you're a guest," Mischa said.

Max was confident, and a little arrogant; he was fat from two decades of being cared for like a guest in the Compound's largest cottage. So he finally mentioned the past that had always angered him. "Who threw me into the jungle?" he said. "Who threw me to the beasts, even though I was defenseless? I would ask you these questions, but the fact is that I already know the answer. I know who was responsible for my misery." He stood up on the velvet seat of his dining-room chair. "You," he pointed dramatically to Esther the White, "you are the one." Max sat once more, and watched Esther the White for a reaction. He lit a cigar and the smoke spiraled in a thin blue stream across the mirror on the dining-room wall.

"Max," Mischa's tone softened, "let bygones be bygones."

So far, Esther the White had ignored Max's attack; she hadn't had much of a choice when she had led Max by the hand to the docks where the circus stood. And if it meant coming to New York, if it meant buying the Compound, and watching the green stone beach from her window, she would do it all again. She would have sold him to the circus again in a minute.

"Then listen to me," Max said to Mischa. "Take my advice and push even farther than Solomon Rath. We'll double our profits if we sell everything now. The houses, all the beach rights. I never got along with Esther the White, it's true: we have a past that divides us. We could split up. Fort Lauderdale, Miami, Los Angeles. Everyone goes where he wants to go."

"I would just like to say," Esther the Black said, "that Ira and I are getting married."

"First you sell the houses, beachfront, with a water view. Then you drain the harbor and sell more houses, beachfront, with a water view," Max said dreamily.

Rose shushed her daughter. "We all know that you'll marry Ira someday."

"But right away," Esther the Black insisted, as she wondered what Phillip's reaction might be once he heard that the harbor he loved might be drained, so that new houses could border the sea wall. "Next month," Esther the Black cried, "we've set a date."

Rose brightened. "Did you hear that, Mother?" she said to Esther the White. "They've made it official." She clapped her hands. "We must talk about the wedding."

"Who gives a damn about the wedding?" Mischa said.

"But bands and halls and flowers have to be reserved," Rose said. And as her mother spoke excitedly, Esther the Black looked around the table, and knew that she could forget her plan—the trousseau money she had dreamed of spending on plane tickets now seemed unobtainable.

"Rose," Esther the White said, slowly, as if she spoke to a child, "this isn't the time."

"You're goddamn right this isn't the time," Mischa shouted. "And I'm not so certain that I would allow that wedding to take place." Esther the Black's eyes widened; she had always believed that was the one thing her family had wanted from her—a good, safe marriage to the accountant's son. "If you want to mention someone who throws people into the jungle, then just mention Solomon Rath."

"Really?" Pagan Rath asked.

"If you want to know who's bleeding me of every cent I ever had, because my wife signed everything over to him, ask your father," Mischa said to Pagan. He then turned to Esther the White. "Rath told me about it when he brought the papers he had signed with Gardner for me to see. Esther," he said, "how could you?"

Esther the White shrugged. "I trusted him," she said.

"You always were so smart," Mischa said. "I could always depend on you."

Cohen suddenly turned to Mischa. "What about the fishermen?" he asked.

"To hell with them," Max said.

"Let them find another beach to ruin," Mischa agreed.

"They're just going to disappear?" Cohen said.

"Since when are you so interested in the poachers? Since when is it your business?" Mischa scowled.

Cohen pushed his chair away from the table. "I am the guard," he said.

"And since you never did such a good job, you should be thankful," Mischa said.

Cohen was standing now, his hands were clenched, his knuckles were white as ice. Who did the brothers think they were, to dispossess nearly thirty people, to make Esther the White so unhappy that she stared unblinkingly at the polished table top. "You better think," Cohen said, "exactly what is going to happen when the fishermen hear about this. I won't be responsible." He waved his arms in the air. "I won't be responsible," he promised.

Cohen turned, and as he left the room Mischa called after him. "Why should you start being responsible now? If you were any kind of a guard the fishermen would have been gone years ago."

Cohen did not turn or answer, but he was wishing he were not so old, that he were a hero, that he could rescue the fishermen and Esther the White, and laugh at the brothers from atop the sea wall.

"That bum," Mischa said, after Cohen had left the room. "Who does he think he is?"

Esther the Black stared into her coffee cup, as if she could find something floating above the sugar and the cream. There would be no money, there would be no escape, the eastern section would be lost, and the green stone beach that Phillip loved. She swallowed and said, "What will happen to my father? What do you think he'll do when he finds out you've sold so much land, that houses will line the beach?"

"He'll have to adjust. He'll have to forget about the drownings," Mischa said.

Esther the White raised her eyes. "What if he can't forget?" she said.

Esther the Black looked across the table. Her grandmother's eyes were watery, and she had pulled the scarf which had hung loosely about her shoulders around her head. Her pale circled eyes stared like those of a gypsy or a ghost.

"We have to think of Phillip," Esther the White said, "of his reaction."

Esther the Black thought that if she stared any longer across the table at the woman she had been named for, the woman whom she never expected to defend Phillip, the lump in her throat would jump like a frog onto the white linen tablecloth. And so, she nodded in agreement with her grandmother, and then she pushed her coffee cup away.

"We won't tell him," Rose said.

"Oh yes we will," Esther the White said, wondering if she should have unlocked the padlock on the sea gate before the beach rights had been sold out from under them.

Pagan Rath leaned across the table and whispered to Esther the Black, "Does this mean our plans are finished?"

Esther the Black nodded. "You can thank your father," she said. "He's stolen everything. He doesn't give a damn if the sale of the beach means my father might try to drown himself again. Blame your father," she said to Pagan, as she went to call a taxi. "And if you ever need money, don't come to me or my family. Go to your father. He's the one who's rich."

Pagan stood up and smiled. "Well, thank you for dinner," he said. But the family did not answer, they were locked in silence, as if they had been caught in a frieze. "The lemon mousse was particularly delicious," he said.

As Esther the Black left to walk Pagan back to the Compound gate, Mischa rose and went to the liquor cabinet. "Why are you sitting here like this?" he said. "What is this, a funeral? It should be a celebration. We'll make some money from Rath's sale." He brought out a decanter of apricot brandy and poured five small glasses full to the brim. "To the sale of the eastern section," he said.

The family raised their glasses and drank a toast with Mischa. All but Esther the White, who sat huddled beneath her blue silk scarf. She did not even hear Mischa when he asked if she would rather have whisky than the sweet brandy. She did not hear because she was struggling; her feet would not remain steady, for under the soles of her shoes, Esther the White felt the Compound slipping, as if the sand moved in circles beneath the dining-room table.

III. BLOODLINES

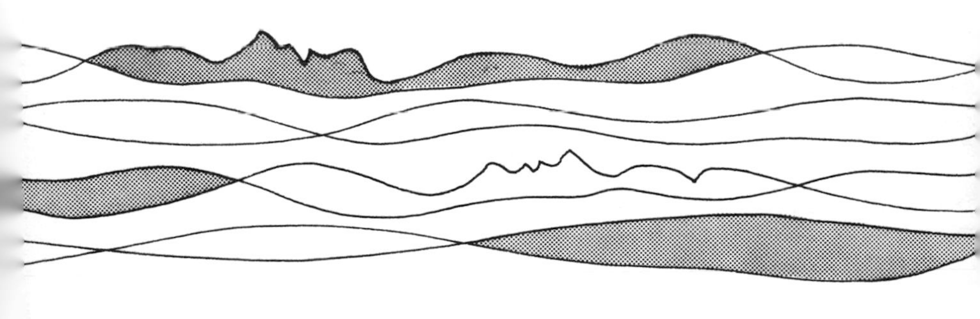

1

Esther the Black and Cohen had the same impulse after Mischa's announcement; and so both eventually found themselves on the path to the fishermen's encampment. But before he crossed the Compound, Cohen had to search his lighthouse for the stolen jade pendant and diamond earrings, which he planned to turn over to the fishermen so that they could fight against the family. He searched through dusty shelves and cluttered drawers; and it was some time before he remembered to rip out the lining of the old sheepskin coat where he had long ago hidden the jewelry, so Esther the Black reached the encampment first. It had been such a long time that Esther the Black had nearly forgotten which way the path turned; and when she appeared in the clearing she felt like a stranger—but nothing had changed, not one grain of sand.

No one seemed to notice her, no one looked up. The fishermen mended fish nets or played cards; only the youngest children, born to women Esther the Black had once played with on the stone beach, stared at her; to them she was a stranger. Esther stood in the shade, beneath a large pine tree; she had no time to lose. When the eastern section was sold, the encampment would be filled with houses and neat yards, and the fishermen would be scattered, to the welfare office, to cheap apartments over the Laundromat in St. Fredrics, the only line binding them together would be the thin blue headbands they wore across their foreheads. Esther the Black refused to be a part of a family that would do such a thing to the fishermen, that would sign the paper allowing every tree, even the one Esther stood beneath, to be leveled.

And she wondered, too, if she was really ready for Phillip's reaction, once he discovered that the beach had been sold. Even though Esther the Black had always longed for the key to the sea wall, she did not want to step over the stones to find her father's imprint in the sand; she did not want him to drown. And so, she searched for Terry; though he had not trusted her when they were lovers, and it was unlikely he would choose to trust her now. She knocked on the screen door of his trailer; inside the table was littered with fishing hooks. Esther the Black felt like crying; but she had no time for anything like that, and she walked right in the door when Terry's wife answered her knock, even though she was not certain she would be able to speak at all.

"Listen," Esther the Black said, ignoring Terry as he began to introduce his wife, his words slow and purposeful, letting Esther know, from the start, that there would never be anything between them again. "There are problems," she told him. "My family has just sold this part of the Compound."

Terry looked at his wife, and then back at Esther. "So?" he said, opening both his palms. "What does it matter to us who owns it? Your family or someone else's family?"

Us, thought Esther the Black; he separates himself and all the fishermen from me right away. "This is different," she said. "This sale is to a land developer. Sam Gardner. He'll knock everything down. You won't be able to stay unless you stop it."

"He'll try," Terry laughed, and he tugged at his blue headband, his talisman, his luck.

"He will," Esther the Black insisted.

"Esther the Black," Terry said, and he offered her a cup of coffee, "you're much too anxious. Relax."

Esther the Black waved Terry's offers away; she turned to his wife. "Believe me," she said, "I want what's best for you."

The woman smiled. "That's hard to believe," she said. "And it would be stupid of you, if it was true. They're your family. You should think about them."

Esther the Black felt guilty; she didn't bother to protest—because it was true, she was thinking about her own family, her father, herself. But it was also true that she thought about the mimosa trees that would fall, the campground that would be leveled, the sea that would never be used for anything more than bathing. She shrugged her shoulders and reached for the trailer door.

"Have some coffee," Terry called to her, but Esther the Black shook her head, and walked down the trailer steps; and as she left she heard his wife call her the Drowned Man's daughter—and it was true, that was who she was. She could not save the eastern section without the fishermen's help, but she might be able to save her father. If she could get hold of enough money to free both her parents from the Compound before the devastation began, Phillip might never know that his beach was sold, he might never care, he could walk along the strip in Las Vegas with no thoughts of water or drowning at all.

Esther the Black crossed over to her side of the Compound; she quietly went up the stairs in her parents' house. When she reached her second-floor bedroom, she went to her window and watched the movements of the night harbor, for she could not sleep that night, and each time the tide moved she imagined she could hear Phillip's cry.

Soon after Esther the Black left the fishermen's campground, Cohen arrived dressed in a sleeveless T-shirt and baggy gray work pants; he waved his arms like a screaming scarecrow in the center of the encampment. A few children turned to stare at him, but Cohen was a familiar figure in the campground, and the fishermen ignored him. The landscape artist had made an anguished decision; he would sell the pendant and earrings, and do whatever he could to stop the sale of the eastern section, he would do it for Esther the White. And so, when his entrance was ignored, Cohen dropped his arms and hiked up his pants. "What's wrong with you people?" he said. "Didn't you hear me?"

"Old man," a boy of fifteen said to Cohen, "be quiet. There's a Bolo game being played." He pointed to a group of gamblers.

"Don't call me old man," Cohen said. "Don't you hear me?" he called to the Bolo players. "They've sold the eastern section."

Cohen stood there, amazed that there had been no reaction to his announcement; without the fishermen he was lost; the jewels would not bring enough cash to buy back the land, but it would buy guns, ammunition, and perhaps enough fear to scare Gardner away forever. Cohen was silent until an old fisherman, a Bolo expert who was now waiting his turn at the game, motioned the landscape artist to join the circle of players. "Listen to me," said the old man, who was no longer able to fish, the outdoor work and winter salt had turned his fingers scaly and hard with arthritis. "That family can't steal this land from us." As the old man spoke, he didn't move his eyes from the Bolo game; he watched only his opponent's hands as pieces of the white skeleton came together. "This place is ours."

"Maybe you're too old to hear right," Cohen said. "It's not yours. They've sold it." He clapped his hands together. "Poof. Like that. Gone."

All the players heard Cohen, they couldn't help but hear him; but no one answered, no one spoke.

"Feh," Cohen muttered. "Cowards," he said.

The old man who was waiting his turn said, "You don't understand. When the family is dead and buried, when they're in the earth, we'll still be here. We've always been here."

"This time it's different," Cohen insisted. "It's not another family who's buying the land. It's a developer."

The old man's opponent fumbled with the bones of the gill. The fisherman smiled; but, before he took his turn at the game, he placed a stiff hand on Cohen's bare arm. "We're still here," he said.

Cohen was disgusted. With the fishermen, with the family, with himself. He left the Bolo players to get a cup of coffee from a large pot simmering on a kerosene stove in the center of the campground. He wondered what he really had; everything he wanted belonged to Mischa. With only a few words and his signature, Mischa could make the eastern section disappear, he could turn Esther the White ashen at the dinner table, he could even decide to take her away. It was as Cohen was drinking hot, black coffee, as he was wrapping his despair around him like a mohair blanket, that he saw a group of young men and women gathering outside a metal trailer. Youth: he thought. He narrowed his eyes, and sucked on his upper lip.

"Hey, you," Cohen called to a man who spoke to the gathering. "You," Cohen repeated. "What's your name?"

"Terry," said the fisherman, who was now repeating what Esther the Black had told him.

"And you?" he pointed to another young man.

"Daniel," the fisherman said. "What's it to you?"

Cohen sat on a weather-beaten log. "I'm just interested," Cohen said. "I'm interested in whether or not you want to stay here, by this harbor."

"What's your point? Get to the point," Daniel said.

"The eastern section has been sold by the family," Cohen said, and he wondered what sort of reaction he would get this time.

"So what?" Terry called to him. "It's been sold before."

Cohen shook his head; young men had no fire anymore. But a young woman, who was not much older than Esther the Black, spoke to him. "What are we supposed to do?" she asked. "We have no legal rights."

Cohen nodded; he should have known to address himself to a woman. "All you have are moral rights," he said.

"What good are moral rights against bulldozers?" the woman asked.

Fire: Cohen smiled. "Guns are good against bulldozers," he said.

Men and women began to leave Terry's trailer door; they gathered around Cohen's log. But he did not speak; he lit a cigarette and waited until there was quiet, until pulses were waiting for him to continue. Cohen shook off his blanket of helplessness; before him was the image of Esther the White's face, the high cheekbones, the arch of her neck when she strained to see the harbor from her window. He could win her, he thought, if he presented her with the eastern section. And, if Mischa was ruined without the sale of the land, what would prevent her from leaving her husband? And she would leave with Cohen, only with Cohen.

"All you have to do is leave it to me," Cohen said. "I can supply you with the money for guns."

"Why should you listen to him?" Terry called from his trailer. "Someone can get murdered, and it will probably be one of us who is that someone."

"Who said murder?" Cohen answered. "Aggravation,

trouble. Resistance doesn't mean murder. Bullet holes in the tires of the bulldozers, that's resistance."

"All right," the young woman near Cohen said. "I'm ready."

Cohen imagined himself parking the Caddy at the door of the gun shop on Route 16. He would leave the engine running, the young woman would be at the wheel, and he would wear suspenders and glasses, no one would suspect him of being a revolutionary; he would look like an old man. And outside, the woman would be waiting in the car, the engine would be running, gas would rise in the dark air.

Cohen threw his cigarette on the ground and stamped it out with his work boot. Idiot, he thought to himself. Don't even imagine that, he thought. That's how they all get caught even before the revolution gets going, they're caught stealing a sock or a shoe, cans of soup in the market, or guns and bullets. He was an old man, too old to run around with stolen ammunition. He would pawn Esther the White's jewelry, and buy the guns outright. Not romantic, Cohen thought, but effective.

"Tell me," a young man asked. "How do you come by enough money for guns?"

"Don't you worry," Cohen said, as he rose. "How I get the money is my business, and then I leave the rest to you."

Cohen walked away, down one of the paths which led from the eastern section to his lighthouse. After he left, the young men and women of the camp continued arguing and dreaming of their revolution under the mimosa trees, under the stars. Cohen himself was dreaming of a woman's face. In the lighthouse, he balanced the sheepskin coat on his knees and slit the lining with a carving knife. The jade pendant which Esther the White had stolen years before fell with a thud onto the hard wooden floor. Even in the gray twilight and dust, the red gold shone like a woman's heart.

Esther the Black, up in her dark bedroom, had no way of knowing what Cohen planned to do; she could not see how he reached down and picked up the pendant, how he stroked the cold jade and gold until the stone was warm. Cohen stared at the carved image in the stone until he had erased all of the jeweler's original lines, until the image was his own. And then, as if imagining alone could exhaust, Cohen placed his head on the table and fell asleep, his fingers holding tightly to the pendant, his head resting in dust.

By morning, Esther the Black was nearly frantic; she hadn't slept, she had no plans, nowhere to turn, and no friend, save Ira Rath. So she hunched over the telephone in her grandparents' hallway, and she dialed Solomon Rath's number—he was a traitor to her family, but Esther the Black swallowed her pride, and when the accountant answered her call she asked for his son.

Solomon Rath sighed heavily. "Don't mention that stinker's name to me. In fact I don't know what his name is anymore. He tells me he changed it. I think he calls himself Savage."

"All right," Esther the Black agreed. "But just let me talk to him."

"Why should I?" the accountant said. "Wasn't it you who convinced him that I ruined your family's fortune? Even though the truth is your family could have ruined themselves quick enough without me—your grandfather should go down on his knees to thank me for finding a buyer for that piece of sand he calls the eastern section. If I take my cut—why shouldn't I? I'm a professional."

"Please," Esther the Black said. "Ira has always been my friend—I would like to talk to him."

"Well, that's impossible," Solomon Rath said. "Because he's not here. He moved into a tenement on Tenth Avenue this morning, and I hope he stays there. I thought you were a sensible girl, Esther. I thought at least you would realize that whatever money I take from the sale of the eastern section would have gone right back to you if you had married my son. But, no. You couldn't see that far. I'm not one to accuse—but now you have forced a young boy to leave his beautiful home for the streets."

"The streets?" Esther asked. "But he has an apartment."

"A slum."

Esther the Black pleaded, and finally Solomon Rath told her where his son now lived—she jotted down the address and thanked the accountant.

"He says music is his life," Rath said. "He says I would never understand. But tell him, tell him, Esther, that he would never understand me either."

Esther the Black hung up the phone, understanding only that Solomon Rath had disrupted every member of her family—and that by selling the land he might be driving her father to another suicide attempt while the beach was still empty enough for him to race over the stones. So, she forgot Rath's plea to his son, and she grabbed the extra set of car keys from the table drawer in the entrance hall of her grandparents' house. She had no time to lose—she ran—and she felt that she was still racing when she started the Caddy and drove through the Compound gates.

Esther's foot was heavy on the accelerator as she drove down Route 16; the tires bounced off curbs as she turned corners. She parked the Caddy at the docks, near the entrance to the ferry. Esther's fingers clutched the steering wheel; and when she finally turned off the engine, she was tired, suddenly tired from racing through the Compound, through town, racing toward a man who might not be able to help her, who might not want to. But she got out anyway; she didn't bother to stop at Woolworth's and report her absence—there was no longer the time to earn money slowly. She had to move quickly—even if she moved toward Ira Rath to beg for money, to beg for a plan. So, Esther the Black left her grandfather's Cadillac in the ferry parking lot; the keys were still in the ignition when she bought a one-way ticket to Manhattan.

When Esther the Black stepped onto the ferry, she was not certain if she would ever be able to return—she was not certain that she could bear to walk beneath her grandmother's cold gaze one more time, or that she would be able to stand by when they finally told Phillip that he would have to remain locked in his cottage all season long. And when the whistle blew, when the ferry's ropes were loosened, and then dropped from the dock's railings, Esther the Black set off for New York City, and territory as foreign as she could find.

2

Soon after the St. Fredrics police discovered the abandoned Cadillac, they began to peer into parked cars on deserted roads and lanes; they questioned transient sailors drifting through town. After they had dragged the harbor and still had not found Esther the Black, Mischa decided that it was time for Phillip to be let out of his cottage. It was time for him to face reality—Phillip's daughter was missing, and his wife was frantic, for Rose had convinced herself that if Esther the Black had not been murdered or kidnapped, then she was surely fighting for her life and breath on some empty beach.

But Phillip only shrugged when Mischa unlocked his cottage and informed him of Esther's disappearance.

"She's quite sensible," Phillip said. "I would never consider her a missing person."

Then Phillip turned away from his father, and went off toward the harbor; he pulled a painted lawn chair close to the sea wall, so that his sneakers rested on the uneven blocks of sandstone, and he breathed in the sea air. He drowsed in the sun. Mosquitoes drifted about his hair in a slow circle. And as Phillip began to fall asleep, as the tide came in, covering the driftwood and the green stones, Esther the White decided that she wanted to do more than dream about her son: she would talk to him. Ignoring the pain in her side, she walked across the wide, green lawn, afraid that now she had lost her granddaughter the same way she had lost Phillip. Without ever having had her—with no shared memories and without a trace.

When Esther the White reached Phillip's chair, she tapped his shoulder.

"Wake up," she said to him, because his yellow eyes were vacant and wide, and Esther the White could tell he had been dreaming. Perhaps of the past.

Phillip looked up and shaded his eyes. "How about a match?" he said, and he took a filtered cigarette from his shirt pocket.

Esther the White held a lit match for her son. Across the lawn the sun moved lower in the sky; it was August, and Drowning Season was nearly over; the days grew shorter. Esther the White's own eyes began to close; she had taken her new prescription for Demerol, and the drug followed her like shadows; she nearly forgot that she had come to the sea wall to tell Phillip that the beach he loved would soon be crowded with houses, and that the water which called to him would be as calm as a bathtub, each wave carrying a swimmer or a body surfer.

"Are you here for a reason?" Phillip asked his mother, surprised that she would come and see him, even though it was his first afternoon out.

Above them the gulls circled high, scavengers cloaked and hidden in white feathers. "Yes," Esther the White said, wondering just how long the guilt for Phillip's childhood would sit like a stone inside of her, in her stomach, in her throat, in the blood which moved through her. "Yes," Esther said. "I've come to tell you that I'm dying."

Her own words surprised her, and Esther the White closed her mouth tightly. Phillip was looking at her, quite clearly, with his deep yellow eyes, and Esther could no longer remember if Solo had really had eyes like that or not. After all these years, she could not remember. "Well." Phillip smiled. "Isn't everybody?"

Esther lit herself a cigarette. "I'm dying faster than others. I have cancer. No one knows." She had expected to speak of Esther the Black's disappearance, she had expected to tell Phillip about the sale of the eastern section. She had never intended to speak out her own fear. She wondered if she was searching for sympathy, an end to her guilt, a final release; but it was too late to wonder why, she had already spoken, and Phillip gazed at the sea wall and nodded solemnly. "I'm sorry," he said.

"Are you?" Esther the White asked. "Are you really?" What if, Esther the White now thought, I had pretended to love him? What if the nursemaid hadn't held his head under water for so long? Would he have hated me anyway? The pain in her side was moving like cold fire, the Demerol made her vision blurry, as if, when she stared at Phillip, he was only an old photograph. Now that the girl was gone, it finally seemed time to ask the question Esther the White had always kept quiet. "Why did you call her Esther?"

"It's a perfectly lovely name," Phillip said, putting out his cigarette and signaling that he wanted another one lit. Like an inmate or an arsonist, Phillip was not allowed to carry matches. Although anyone could have told Mischa that Phillip was not at all interested in fire; that was not his element.

"A million other names are lovely," Esther the White pressed him.

"That's true," Phillip said. "Cathleen is quite nice. Also Sally. And Marion and Jane."

"You called her by my name," Esther the White said. "Mine."

"I wanted to, that's all," Phillip whined.

"Oh, stop it," Esther the White said. She wanted to know, she needed to know, and she might not have another chance to ask. "Stop being such a child."

Phillip looked at her shrewdly. "Then stop treating me like one. You never liked children, dear. So, give it up. And you can start by giving me my own matches."

Esther the White stared at the harbor; in the glare of the sunlight the water was nearly invisible. She wished she could have loved him. And she shivered, even though the sun was strong. Her eyes were cloudy, her eyes were damp; she was very close to tears, too close.

"Give it up, old girl," Phillip said softly, the softest words he had ever said to her.

Esther the White quickly wiped her eyes with her silk scarf; she handed Phillip a pack of matches.

"Success without college," Phillip read from the cover. He laughed, lit his cigarette, and tucked the matchbook into his shirt pocket. "Maybe that was the core of my problem," he said, in the hope of changing the conversation to a lighter tone. "I didn't get this matchbook's advice when I most needed it in life."

Esther the White stared at her son. "That still doesn't tell me why you gave her my name," she said.

Phillip puffed on his cigarette; smoke rings hid his face, his wild, yellow eyes. "I named my child Esther," he finally said, when the gulls were reaching into the water and crying out to each other above the shoreline, "because I knew you would hate that. You would hate her. And I wanted to steal from you, to turn you into a ghost."

Esther the White nodded; her silk scarf blew like a veil in the wind. Her eyes burned, but she still stared at her son, shielding her vision with her hand, watching as Phillip seemed to grow older by the second, right before her eyes.

"And, anyway," Phillip said now, "Esther the Black is also my ghost. It's interesting how that happened, but it's true. We have the same ghost." He smiled.

"The girl is missing," Esther the White said. "You call her your ghost, but you don't seem haunted. You don't seem concerned. You just sit here by your wall, and stare out at your harbor. Not very concerned." Esther the White shook her head.

"I don't consider her missing, just because she is not in the Compound. But I do consider her unwanted. Unloved. There are things worse than missing, you know," Phillip said. "There are things which force a ghost to haunt you forever."

Esther the White did not hear Phillip's words. She was remembering the day she stood outside her parents' small house; it was years before the strand of beads had broken onto the floor, years before Esther noticed that her eyes were a clear, hard blue. It was soon after her tenth birthday, and an early spring had suddenly come. Some of the snow had already begun to melt; up above, in the mountains, the wolves howled at dawn, as if howling alone could bring back the snow that kept tracks secret and covered.

That day, Esther the White had been sent to the river for water. The ice closest to the shore had melted, and Esther carried a large bucket hooked over her shoulders with a thick, brown rope. She wore a woolly dress which scratched her knees, and blue ribbons tied around her braids. But the day was too warm for carrying buckets, so Esther the White walked past the riverbank; she trudged through the dark muddy earth, up toward the hills which led to the mountains. She was not yet afraid of wolves, or of being alone; and because winter had suddenly, magically disappeared, Esther the White walked farther away from the village than she ever had before.

When she reached the first hilltop, Esther the White thought she heard voices, but there was no one around. Perhaps it was only an echo from the mountain above, the one they called the Wild Dog, because the crevices looked like fangs, and the snow on the peak looked like the foam around the mouth of a mad dog. Still, Esther the White heard voices, and when she walked a little farther she saw a sixteen-year-old girl from the village. Esther breathed easier; there were no Cossacks or robbers or gypsies, only Rifka, who wore a long fur cape, even though the day was warm and the birds had already begun to return from the south. Rifka turned around before Esther the White had time to smile or call out.

"What are you doing here?" Rifka said. Her deep red hair hung to her waist; her face was white and drawn. Esther knew that she had spent the winter inside her parents' house complaining of aches and refusing to meet with her cousin, Lazar, who came every evening to see her. "What are you doing here?" Rifka said again. Her voice was as soft as a snake's, and she waved a heavy cotton scarf in the air. "There are wolves here," she said.

"There are not," Esther the White argued. "The only wolves are up there." She pointed to the Wild Dog. It was when Esther lifed her arm to point to the mountaintop that she noticed the blood on Rifka's scarf. But she didn't say anything, not one word. She looked down at the mud puddles around her boots.

"Yes," Rifka insisted. "There are too wolves here. They come at night, like ghosts, when everyone is in bed."

Esther the White felt her skin crawl. There was a bundle on the earth, resting near the hem of Rifka's cape.

"You'd better go right away," Rifka suggested.

"What's that?" Esther the White said, pointing to the bundle.

"What?" Rifka said.

"That." Esther pointed to what looked like a heap of rags; but something was moving on the damp, still-cold earth.

Rifka moved away. Esther the White could see a tiny child; an infant's arms and legs waved, an infant's voice cried when Rifka moved away. But the cry was weak and no one else could have heard it, except maybe the wolves.

"Whose is that?" Esther the White asked.

Rifka was standing near her now; her hair was so long that, when she turned to look back, the tips of her hair touched Esther's face and streaked across her skin like feathery blood.

"Nobody's," Rifka said, though they could both hear the baby cry. "It's nobody's, and don't you dare tell anybody what you saw, Esther the White," Rifka said. "Do you understand?"

Esther the White could not stop staring.

"Do you understand?" Rifka pulled a braid of Esther the White's hair, and then she went back and tucked the bundle beneath a low bush. Rifka smoothed her hair, and she pinched her pale cheeks to bring the color back. She took Esther the White's hand and led her away.

"Do you think anyone will find it?" Esther the White asked.

Rifka pinched her skin harder. They walked down to the river together; Rifka waited as Esther the White filled up her bucket. When they entered the village, each one would return to her own mother. Rifka's mother would shake her head when Rifka told her she was sick again; and when the girl went up to the sleeping loft where she would face the wall with empty eyes and pale cheeks, her mother would shake her head again, and wonder if such a sickly girl would ever find a husband.

Esther the White's mother would scold her for taking so long with the water; she might even smack Esther's face with the back of her hand. The two girls thought about their mothers as they walked down the dirt road which wound through the village; their feet slipped in the mud, and the water that Esther carried sloshed over the bucket and onto her shoulders.

"Rifka," Esther the White said, and she thought about the blood she had seen on Rifka's scarf, "did it hurt? Was it terrible?"

Rifka held a finger to her lips. They had neared Esther's house; her mother stood on the porch, waiting and tapping her foot. "Yes," Rifka whispered. "Terrible."

Esther the White watched after Rifka; but Rifka walked straight ahead. She didn't look back toward the hills, not once. And that night, sleeping in a bed between her brothers, Esther the White heard the wolves howling up above. The moon was very bright, and Esther could think of nothing but the baby sleeping under a small leafless bush. For several nights afterward, Esther dreamed of babies, of children lost in the woods. She wondered if Rifka also had these dreams. When Esther's family visited one night in Rifka's parents' house, Rifka's eyes were bright, and she did not even look in Esther's direction; her cheeks were pink as rose petals.

Esther the White tried hard to believe that someone would find the infant—a childless woman from the village, a gypsy, or a nobleman. But the wolves still howled at night, and the weather changed again, so that the false spring disappeared, and the puddles of earth and water turned to ice once more. It was then that Esther the White decided that she herself would go back to the hill and find the child. Her own mother could raise it; the child would be a brother or a sister to Esther; perhaps, when she herself married, she would take the child with her to her own house. Or, perhaps Rifka would decide she had made a terrible mistake, and thank Esther with kisses and tears when the baby was returned.

And so, one morning, Esther the White returned to the hillside where she had first seen Rifka. It was not winter or spring, but some gray time in between. The hillside was quiet, and the peak of the Wild Dog was covered in clouds, so that it looked as if there were no mountain towering darkly over the village and the river and hills. Esther could not find the child. She looked for quite a long time, wondering if an infant wrapped in rags might have rolled downhill, or if it had somehow managed to crawl away. But there was no sign that the child had ever been there; even the rags were gone. There were no footprints in the ice which had formed on the hillside—not the mark of a woman, nor the pawprint of a wolf. And Esther the White sat down on the cold, hard earth and wondered if somewhere the child was crying; and she shivered as if it were she who had been left alone in the woods, unprotected and waiting for any approaching step.

By the time she herself was pregnant, Esther the White had long forgotten that lost child of Rifka's. But now this talk of ghosts had suddenly made her remember, and she felt the loss more strongly than ever. She looked at her son as if he had been the child bundled in rags and left on the ice. On this August afternoon, all Esther the White saw was a stranger, a man who looked old, whose beard was gray, not at all her child, the thin, pale boy with the water-soaked hair.

"I should have loved you," Esther the White said.

"It's too late for that now," Phillip said. "Why don't you try loving your granddaughter? I want her to have something; I want my daughter to be different, to be loved. You know, Mother," he lowered his voice, "I really am your child. I can't love."

Esther the White looked down, at the earth; he was right, he was her son, whether Mischa was his father or not, he was hers, and she had never been able to see it before. She felt that she owed him something, if only because he was hers. "I came here to tell you that your father and Max have decided to sell the eastern section of the Compound. Max is trying to convince your father to sell everything. I am trying to convince him not to."

Phillip stared at her quietly; he looked sane—an old, sane stranger. "Have they done that?" he said. "Really?"

"I had no way to stop them."

"Of course not," Phillip said. "Well, that's the end of my harbor. Not even a place to haunt."

"You're not surprised?" Esther asked; she had been truly frightened of his reaction, she had imagined that he would jump from his chair to climb the sea wall one last time.

"I've given that up, too," Phillip said. "Surprise, hate, all of it."

His hands were so frail that Esther wondered how they helped him climb the sea wall; she wondered if they were strong enough to make another attempt that season.

"I want to do something," Esther the White said. "I want to be something to her. But it's too late for that."

"Never," Phillip said. "No such thing as too late."

"I can't do anything." Esther the White dropped her closed hands on her lap. "I'm dying," she said.

"Yes, you're dying," Phillip said. "But you're not dead."

Esther the White closed her eyes. "I'll try," she said.

"Do," Phillip said, leaning back in his lawn chair with a satisfied smile. "I'm feeling much more relaxed now." And it was true, his eyes were heavy with Valium and sun. "Do something, and then we might all be able to give up our ghosts," he said now, but he didn't look at Esther the White, and she was uncertain that he had even spoken the words. "Look," he said, as his analyst, Dr. Otto, drove through the Compound gate in his MG. "The man's pathetic," Phillip confided to Esther. "But I enjoy confusing him. Just when he thinks he has me pegged—when he figures my case is closed, I invent new symptoms. The sessions amuse me."

Phillip nodded as the psychiatrist walked across the green toward them.

Dr. Otto reached down and shook Esther the White's hand.

"Doctor," Phillip said, "have you met the woman who pretends to be my mother?"

The psychiatrist shook Esther's hand with the grip of a co-conspirator, but Esther the White was not on his side; she never had been. "I'll go now," she told Phillip.

"Must you?" Dr. Otto said, as he removed his driving gloves. "I thought that as long as you're right here, we might try some confrontation therapy. That might just lead us to the core of your son's problems."

"Alleged son," Phillip said.

"Actually," Esther the White said, as she rose from the lawn as gracefully as she could, though the pain in her stomach was shifting like a wave and she really did not want to leave Phillip's side, "the core of my own problem is the need for a nap."

As Esther the White walked across the lawn, she heard Phillip's laughter and the light, sweet sound settled inside her as it echoed above the Compound. Alleged son, alleged bastard, alleged lunatic; Phillip's laughter was growing inside of her, fluttering like a bird.

Esther the White had no real money of her own—Solomon Rath was in control of that—but she did have the jade pendant hidden somewhere in the pine grove, and that could bring several thousand dollars. She would give the jade pendant to Esther the Black, as soon as the girl returned to the Compound. Then Esther the Black would have options in her life, and more: she would trust Esther the White, she would love her, remember her.

She wished she had had something to give before, when

Phillip was young; but it was not too late. First, she must find Cohen and get a shovel or a spade. They would dig up the entire pine grove if they had to. But, when she reached the porch of the main house, Esther the White had to stop. Her head was light, her stomach was filled with icy air, and the pain was heavier than the earth she would have to dig.

Esther the White walked into the dark hallway of her house; when she reached the stairs, she held onto the banister and counted backward from one hundred, a method she had been using since the pain began. But today she could no longer count backward, she could not remember what number followed eighty-six, she could not even feel the wooden banister beneath her hand.

Esther the White did not carry a shovel to the pine grove that day; she did not call Cohen. Instead, she walked up the stairs and into her room; she locked the door behind her and crushed Demerol into a glass of warm fruit juice she had left on her bureau. As the pain was dulled, as the Demerol moved through her bloodstream, Esther the White silently thanked Phillip for allowing her another chance, for convincing her she still had something to give. True, the girl had disappeared, but Esther the White had nothing to worry about; Esther the Black would return; she had to. That was all there was to it. All through the night Esther the White slept dreamlessly, although, when she awoke, she could have sworn she had been dreaming of something sweet.

3

In the morning, Cohen's plans were disrupted. He had hoped to catch the ferry to Manhattan, where he would sell the jade pendant, and perhaps the small earrings as well, and buy shotguns; instead, he found a note from Esther the White asking him to meet her at the shed. Esther the White was waiting for him under a pine tree, her sunglasses were tilted far back on her white hair, and she held a shovel in her hand.

"As usual," she said, "whatever goes on between us is private."

Cohen swallowed; the jade pendant, hidden in his work boot, began to burn through the bone of his shin. "It's too hot a day to be working outside, let's go in and have a glass of lemonade. Tea is good on a day like this—it warms up your intestines, so they don't know whether they're coming or going."

Esther the White shook her head. "My granddaughter's missing, did you know that?" she asked.

Cohen waved his hand in the air. "Don't worry," he said. "She's probably with her Ira Rath. Although, maybe you should worry; I'm not too crazy about him."

Esther the White now thought of her decision, such a long time ago, to bury the past in the earth, to forget her own childhood and let the Compound honeysuckle—its odor so strong it had hung over the ice as Esther the White's fingers cracked with the cold as she buried the jewels—take over everything, even her memory. And now, as she stood with Cohen by her side, the odor of that same flower filled her, as if memory and pain could both be erased with a flower, with a scent.

Cohen wanted more than anything to get Esther the White away from the pine grove; he needed time—time to get to the city, pawn the jade stone, and rescue the eastern section. He took the shovel from Esther's hand and held her shoulder lightly. "Pretty soon your husband may decide to sell the rest of the Compound. I'm old, I won't have a job anymore, I'll have to sit around and watch flowers grow like a bluejay. So, let's take a rest. Why should we hurry around on such a hot day?" He sat on a large stone and rested the shovel on the ground.

"Listen to me," Esther the White said, and she seemed to tower above him, her shadow covered him. "I want to give my granddaughter something. That time I buried a stone, a jewel in the pine grove. It's worth quite a lot. Esther the Black can go to Europe, she can go to college, she can do whatever she wants to do."

Cohen closed his eyes. Why now? he thought. After all these years, why does she need to look for it now? "A jewel?" he said.

"That's right," Esther nodded.

"Worth quite a lot?" he repeated. And when Esther nodded, he said, "Why wouldn't you use it yourself?" He cleared his throat, swallowing was like chewing dust. "You could sell the jewel and leave the Compound."

"Leave?" Esther the White said. "I'm too old for that." She narrowed her eyes. "Why would I ever want to leave here? I spent my whole life trying to get here."

"I was afraid you would leave," Cohen said softly. "I was always afraid."

"Cohen," Esther the White said. "I have to admit that I don't remember where I buried it."

She was not about to leave him; still, he had promised the fishermen guns, and he would have to let her know the truth—that he had stolen from her, that he had kept the jewels captive all this time.

"Cohen," she was saying. "Do you remember?"

Cohen shrugged his shoulders. "I have to think," he said.

Esther the White sat next to Cohen and sighed. "I'm tired," she said.

"It's the heat," Cohen told her. He wondered what was happening; why Esther the White had suddenly decided to look for the jewels; why they should be sitting together on a large gray rock on an August afternoon. But, the woman who sat next to him lighting a cigarette and coughing gently had white hair, and he himself was nearly bald; there was no time to figure out what to do next. He merely spoke. "Listen," he said. "I don't have much time. The Compound is dropping to its knees—soon your husband will need a landscape artist like he needs a hole in the head. I'm an old man," Cohen said, and then he corrected himself. "I'm almost an old man." He fumbled for words, he did not look her in the eyes. "Listen," Cohen said quickly, "maybe you should marry me."

Esther the White had been thinking of Esther the Black's look of surprise when she received the jade pendant; when Cohen spoke, Esther the White gripped one hand with the other; the pale blue veins in her wrist turned violet. She spoke like a dreamer. "But, I'm already married," she said.

Cohen lit a cigarette, he waved the smoke in the air. "All right," he said. "We could just live together. Nowadays that's done all the time. And frankly, I don't need the government to have a record of my life. But think about it, because I certainly think we should be together."

"Why?" Esther the White said.

"Why?" Cohen repeated. "Because we should do it. We should have done it a long time ago."

Cohen's words echoed in his head; it was as if someone else had spoken them, someone else had screamed them in the vacuum of the pine grove. Both Esther and Cohen were silent, embarrassed; some lunatic, some crazy man had just ripped their mutual silence with his teeth, and Esther and Cohen were now politely ignoring the wounds.

Esther the White could not help but wonder what might have happened if Cohen had spoken these same words years before, when they were still young, when she first began to know that Cohen stayed at the Compound because of her.

"I don't know," Esther the White said softly.

Cohen was ready to take any word from Esther the White as encouragement. "You're not a snob," he said. "I don't think it means a thing to you that your husband pays my salary. It's true," Cohen shrugged, "he hasn't paid me in months."

Esther nodded; Cohen was a gentleman, who else would have stayed on at the Compound? The pain began again in her left side, and she pushed hard against her ribs. "I don't know," she said absently. "I'm married."

Esther the White knew that she would have never said yes to him years ago. She would have had to give everything away to love him. Still, she remembered how he had looked that night as he knelt on the ice, as he watched her in the grove of black pine. "It's too late," she said. "Too late."

"Who says?" Cohen demanded.

"Let's go," Esther the White said, smoothing back her pale hair, and reaching for the shovel. "Let me get at least one thing settled."

"Esther," Cohen called. "What would you have said if I had asked before? When we were younger?"

Esther the White smiled and leaned on the shovel. "I might have considered," she lied.

The morning grew later; as Cohen watched Esther the White shovel out earth the heat began to rise until it was obvious that this would be a record-breaking day, and even Esther the White, who was always chilled by the pain that ran through her, removed her sweater and fanned herself with a pale limp hand.

Cohen reached into his boot and walked across the pine grove. His heart was beating, his legs felt stiff. "Esther," he said. Esther the White stopped digging and stood by his side. "I promised the fishermen I would help them fight Gardner and his bulldozers," he said.

"Cohen," Esther the White said, "you didn't."

"I did," Cohen said. "Of course I did. Are the fishermen supposed to drop dead, should they take a midnight train to Miami Beach on your husband's say-so?"

"Please don't say 'your husband,' " Esther the White said; the phrase grated on her nerves.

"Of course," Cohen said, "the fishermen can raise plenty of trouble without my help. I'd like to see the day anyone takes this harbor away from the fishermen."

Esther the White turned from Cohen to stare at the holes she had dug. "I really can't remember," she said to herself.

"You're pretty good with a shovel," Cohen said.

"Do I have a choice?" Esther the White felt tired and hot, and she wished that a rain would fall, or that a tidal wave would wash away the pine grove, and she would simply have to lean down and pluck out the treasure from the earth. She felt certain that it was only the heat which forced Cohen to speak of love. Heat did strange things, Esther the White thought. It might have mixed up Cohen's memory; he was not so young anymore.

And when she turned, from staring at the pine grove, when she was about to ask Cohen one more time if he remembered where he had seen her so long ago, Cohen dropped the jade pendant into Esther the White's hand.

"Just remember," Cohen said to her. "You don't owe me anything. When you decide to marry me, which would be a very good idea, just remember not to do it because you owe me anything."

Esther the White sat down; she had to, she did not think her legs would hold her. She sat in the grove, in the earth, as if she were a child. She did not ask Cohen how he came to have the pendant, she did not thank him; but she began to think his offer stemmed from more than mere memory.

"Cohen," she said, and the landscape artist had to kneel in the earth to hear her voice, "was there a pair of diamond earrings, too?"

Esther the White now wondered if she would even recognize the one gift Solo had given her. She wondered if the small stones were pear-shaped or oval; if they had ever existed at all.

Cohen pulled his beret out of his pants pocket and placed the hat on his head to protect against the sun. But his head was dizzy, light as air. He had always imagined that the diamonds had been a gift from Mischa; or perhaps a lover, perhaps someone Esther the White had once adored. "Do you want there to have been earrings?" he said.

Esther the White answered quickly. "No," she said, not wanting to remember Solo, or the gift he had given her.

"No," said Cohen. "No earrings."

The landscape artist helped Esther to her feet, and as he walked with her across the lawn, she listened to his problems with the fishermen, and she nodded when he explained that he now had to go across to the eastern section. She stayed at the sea wall to watch as he crossed through the pine grove, but Esther the White did not see Cohen toss the diamond earrings over the sea wall, she did not see that they fell among a thousand green stones. And while Esther watched Cohen, as she held the jade pendant in her fingers, she made another decision: she would accept Cohen's offer. She had decided to love him.

Cohen did not know what to expect from the young fishermen when he told them of his decision. He found the group on the beach, drying woven nets on the rocks, discussing the low quality of the mussels in the harbor that season. The heat wave grew stronger; and the women wore halter tops and shorts, their long hair was tied up with the blue headbands in long dark manes.

Cohen sat on a large algae-coated rock that was still cool and wet with the tide.

"So," a young woman who was retying torn strands in a large fishing net said, "here is our hero."

Cohen shrugged. "Not such a hero."

"Please," the young fisherman, Daniel, who had come to sit with Cohen, said. "Why such modesty, Cohen?" He placed his bare feet on the dark, wet rock and opened a paper bag; he had been to the McDonald's on Route 16, and had brought back lunch for nearly everyone on the beach. Daniel ate a hamburger. "If I knew you would be here," he apologized, "I would have picked up something for you." He offered Cohen french fries. "This meal is a celebration, because construction is scheduled to begin tomorrow."

"I can't eat those kinds of hamburgers," Cohen said. "Stomach."

Daniel nodded and chewed. Some of the young men and women came to sit with Cohen; the older fishermen avoided him, and called him troublemaker to themselves. Cohen took off his sleeveless undershirt and mopped his face. He chewed a pale french fry, but it stuck to his throat like paper. He suffered from heat, and sadness, and joy. He wished the fishermen's eyes did not look up at him, expecting his words to drip deliciously about their ears. But he had asked for it, no one had begged him to help.

When he told them there were no guns, could he also explain that he wasn't a traitor, that he did not love the Compound and the eastern section any less? Could he tell them that, for him, Esther the White was the Compound; when he saw her he saw the pine grove in winter, coated in ice, he saw the harbor sand move in the lines of her face, each pale vein contained the scales of harbor fish, and the gardenias he had fed nails to for years were carried in her plain blue scarf.

The young fishermen grew restless. "When do we get the guns? When do we figure out our plans?" one of them asked.

Cohen stared at the clear outline of Connecticut across the Sound. "There aren't any guns," he told them.

"You're kidding?" Daniel said.

"No kidding," Cohen told him. "It didn't work out."

Under a birchwood tree, three old fishermen played Bolo in the shade; when voices on the beach were raised, the old-timers left their fishbones game to see what trouble was stirring.

"You're a traitor," Esther the Black's friend Terry said.

"Are you working against us now?" a woman stopped cleaning mussels to ask. "Are you on the side of the family? How much did they pay you?"

Cohen lowered his eyes; no one could have paid him with more than Esther the White's clear gaze, with the touch of her fingers when he slipped the pendant into her palm.

The oldest fisherman, the Bolo expert who had ignored Cohen in the clearing when he had first made his announcement, pushed his way through the young men and women. He stared at Cohen through sun-small dark eyes. "Don't yell at him," the old man said. "Don't make so much noise. You're like seagulls. Screaming and screaming."

"I promised them guns," Cohen explained to the old man.

"I know," the fisherman said.

"And he didn't get them," a boy of seventeen said accusingly.

"Good," said the old fisherman. "We don't need them." He smiled at Cohen. "But it was a very nice idea. Very romantic. Never would have worked, but romantic."

"What do we do?" Daniel called out. "Just walk away?"

"Yes." The old fisherman squinted in the sun.

"These old men," Daniel said to his friends, "they're as good as dead."

Cohen laughed, because minutes before he had been imagining making love to Esther the White. The old fisherman looked over at him. "Dead?" he said. "Too much the opposite. More alive than you would like to think, boy." He tapped his forehead. "And smart."

"So smart that we just walk away and leave everything behind?" someone called.

"That's right," the old fisherman said. "But I didn't say where we walk to, did I?"

These words silenced the group, which had turned from Cohen. Even the landscape artist was curious. Even he could see a better plan than his gun-running in the old man's smile.

"So?" Cohen asked. "What is your plan?"

The fisherman tapped his head again. In his hand he held a dried fishbone from the Bolo game, and it left traces of sand on his cheek.

"Sorry," he said. "You've got divided loyalties. Let me make it easier for you by saying this plan is only for us."

For a while Cohen sat alone on the wet stone and bathed his feet in the tide, but he felt deserted. So he pulled on his damp undershirt and walked across the beach. He climbed over the sea wall and turned; the fishermen were like shadows under the birchwood tree; they had already forgotten him. Cohen walked across the lawn, thinking that the old fisherman was right—it was better not to know. Some things. Some things it was better to know. Like what was going to happen with his life, with Esther the White. Anything could happen, Cohen thought, as he crossed the wide lawn. Nothing could happen.

At his window, where he had pulled up a soft chair so that he could view the Compound more comfortably, Phillip could see Cohen's shoulders stoop, he could see the rings of sweat on the landscape artist's undershirt. And he could also see his mother sitting on the porch in the fading light. Esther the White sat before a wicker table. "Cohen," she called, and she signaled to him, "I made tea."

"Tea?" Cohen said. He scratched his head and strained to see what expression might be on her face, but her eyes were as pale and as clear as ever.

Phillip moved closer to his window, he pressed his nose against the glass. Across the room Rose watched the TV, but the only thing Phillip wanted to see was the Compound, the way the shadows fell against the trees.

"That's right," Esther the White said, as she poured another cup of tea into a china blue cup. "Peppermint," she said.

Across the Compound, Phillip unearthed his binoculars. He became glued to the window. He could see the movement of Cohen's throat as he gulped hot tea in the last of the sunlight; he could see the seagulls perched in the birch trees and on telephone wires. Phillip smiled when he saw Cohen reach over and touch Esther the White's hand; if his mother was feeling something—now a drowning might mean something to her, a drowning might leave its mark. It was perfect timing, really; but Esther the White's reaction was not the most important thing—it was merely an interesting coincidence. So, Phillip turned his binoculars away from Cohen and Esther the White; he let them have their tea alone, without any outside observer, and he turned his attention to the Compound gates.

He had begun to hear the rumbling as soon as Esther the White informed him of the sale of the eastern section of the Compound. Across the lawn, past the mimosa and the pines, just outside of the iron gate, the bulldozers now began to arrive. Phillip checked his watch. He had calculated that the bulldozers would appear in the evening, near dinnertime, gathering like deer at a cool, dark pool. Not bad, Phillip smiled; his timing had been nearly exact. He stared through his binoculars, far past Esther the White, who now poured honey into the peppermint tea with her fragile, tentative hands. Phillip moved his binoculars closer to the window; he had the senses of a fish—he had heard the bulldozers when they were still invisible to the naked eye, still silent to any other ear. And he sat so silently, so calmly, that he could have surprised any fly that rested on his hot, damp skin with one flick of his tongue.

4

Esther the Black was not trained for the unusual. No one had told her that the sun does not always rise over the harbor, and that all fathers do not try to kill themselves once a year, regularly as clockwork. She could never have imagined that her grandmother spent hours sitting in front of a smoky Italian mirror, practicing a speech she hoped to deliver to Esther the Black when she presented the girl with the jade pendant. Esther the Black would never have guessed that Cohen had decided to lay the fishermen's friendship on the line for the woman he loved—or if, in some romantic hour, Esther the Black could have imagined that much, she would never have guessed that the woman was her own grandmother, Esther the White.

And when she first arrived in Manhattan and walked down Tenth Avenue, she would never have guessed that Ira Rath would fall in love with her. When she went to the apartment where Ira now lived with The Quick and the Mad, Esther the Black had a purpose. She had come to ask for a loan—she was certain the accountant, Solomon Rath, would give in to any whim of Ira's—and if he were asked, the elder Rath could come up with enough cash to settle Phillip and Rose far away from the Compound, before Phillip's drowning impulse was pushed to the limit by the construction that would level the eastern section. So, Esther the Black had knocked on Ira Rath's new front door; she had run a hand through her hair, using her fingers as a comb. She waited in the dark hallway. The lock clicked three times; Ira opened the door.

He stared at her, surprised. "You smell like fish," he said.

"The ferry," Esther the Black explained. "Can I come in?"

"Of course." He motioned her into the apartment. "Please," he said. Esther the Black looked past him, at the huge, old apartment littered with the back-up band, The Quick and the Mad; she hesitated. "Esther," he assured her, "you have picked the perfect night for a visit. Tonight I am famous. I can have the world," he said confidently. "And it never would have happened, if not for you."

"Ira," Esther the Black said, once she was inside, "I came here to ask for help." She spoke loudly, so that she could be heard over the voices of The Quick and the Mad, who were seated on the floor with a bottle of tequila and a sliced grapefruit.

He raised a finger to his lips. "Ssh," he said. "They call me Pagan here. Not even my bass player knows my real name."

Pagan sat on a red leather drum seat. "Esther," he said. "I don't think you understand that I have a hit on my hands. The night I left your family's dinner, I thought about what my father had done—and I realized that if he could steal from your family—I could steal from him. Why should I struggle like every other starving musician, when all I had to do was ask the old man for the cash? He fought me, sure, but I laid it on the line. I told him, 'Pop, you either cough up two grand, or I'll peddle my ass if I have to.' Peddle my ass, that's what I said. He came up with the cash, and we recorded 'Nova Scotia Avenue.' We've got a distributor, and Sam Goody's has already ordered the record. WNEW's been playing the demo. At least twice a day. And I've got no guilt, Esther, thanks to you. None. I walked right out of the old man's apartment yesterday, and when he said, 'How can you leave me after all I've done for you, after I gave you the money to cut your goddamn record,' I turned, and do you know what I said to him?"

Esther the Black swallowed hard. "No," she said.

"I said, 'If I thank anyone it'll be Esther the Black. It was her money and not yours that paid for "Nova Scotia Avenue." I can have the world, Esther," Pagan said. "I'm famous." He sighed.

"Great," Esther the Black said. "Wonderful. But, Ira, the truth is, I need some money too. I've got to get my father away from the Compound before he knows it was sold. Just a couple of hundred," she said. "Just a loan."

Trucks en route to New Jersey shook the street as Esther the Black waited for an answer. Finally, Pagan Rath shook his head. "I'm sorry," he said, "but you've got to understand, the record business is expensive. I've got my agent's fees, a road manager, new outfits for The Quick and the Mad, and my advance for the album we're cutting hasn't come through yet. There's no money, Esther. I thought you understood that. Nothing left now—but soon I'll be rich—soon I can lend you whatever you need. Forget about lending—I'll give it to you."

Esther the Black lit a cigarette and closed her eyes. What

was she doing in an apartment with someone who could have the world, when her own world seemed to be growing smaller by the minute. Esther leaned close to the dingy wall, and she wished that there was some way for her to crawl inside the plaster.

"You're sending out very negative vibes, Esther. Money isn't everything, you know." Pagan Rath swung his suede boots away from the drum set and stood by her. "They're playing my song on WNEW. On the fucking radio."

Esther the Black apologized for her reaction; she wished she could congratulate him on his good luck, but she couldn't, her heart wasn't in it. She ran her fingers up and down the yellow wall; all her plans had turned to dust. She had been fighting the Compound and her grandmother for a lifetime, and now there was no more time, now the eastern section had been sold, and Phillip's reaction might be anything, anything at all.

"I have everything I always wanted," Ira Rath was saying. "Everyone calls me Pagan now. It's like I'm a different person."

One of The Quick and the Mad now suggested that the band celebrate its success at a party going on in Newark. "Let's go, Pagan," the drummer called. "New Jersey is waiting for us."

But Pagan Rath shook his head and turned to Esther. "Stay," he said.

"Me?" Esther the Black said.

"I'm not going to that party in Newark," Pagan Rath said. "I'd rather stay here, with you."

The Quick and the Mad picked up their tequila, their guitars, and their girlfriends; they scuttled out of the apartment, leaving tracks of cigarette ash and success in crazy circles. Esther the Black felt she didn't have a friend in the world; she couldn't face the ferry ride back to St. Fredrics with no success of her own, and no new plans. She decided to stay. She took off her clothes, and agreed to make love with Pagan Rath on a mattress without sheets.

"Sorry," he apologized, "but I've just moved into this apartment, and I haven't had time to go to the Laundromat. This has been a hectic week."

But Esther the Black didn't mind; she sighed, because when Pagan Rath touched her breasts she was able to forget the color of the harbor sand in late morning. And because when he moved inside of her, Esther the Black could no longer hear the owls in the pine grove calling. "Thank you," she said to him when they had finished; but when she reached for her clothes, which lay on the floor near the mattress, Pagan Rath stopped her hand. "You don't have to go," he said. "Don't leave tonight."

Pagan Rath's eyes were tired and red; Esther could see her own reflection in their centers.

"Are you ever afraid of the dark?" Esther the Black asked, thinking of her grandmother's bedroom light, which was always burning, in the latest night, in the earliest morning.

"I'm afraid of 'Nova Scotia Avenue,'" Pagan Rath said.

She told him she would stay, but only till morning. But in the morning, Pagan begged her to accompany him to the recording studio, where The Quick and the Mad were taping their album, *Dog in Pain.*

Esther the Black soon realized that Ira could not get through the recording session without a bottle of Jack Daniels, or without holding her hand.

And later, during lunch at a deli on Seventh Avenue, Pagan asked if she thought she could love him.

"I don't think so," Esther answered.

"I think it might work," Pagan said as he ordered a corned beef sandwich. "I think it could work. You changed my life; you opened my eyes; you taught me that if you want something bad enough you'll take it—even if it comes from your father. You're good for me; I just know it."

"Ira," Esther the Black said, "I can't talk myself into loving you."

Pagan Rath held her hand tightly. "Love can happen if you want it to—if you really try." He stopped and pulled out a notebook from the pocket of his leather jacket. "That's a great lyric," he said. "You see, you inspire me. Come on the road with me. My manager's set up four concert dates in California. You're the only one who really knows me. You're the only one who calls me Ira."

"I don't know," Esther the Black said, although the truth was she would have liked to say yes—she liked the way his tongue moved up and down on her skin, she liked the way he needed her.

"Think about it," Pagan said, and he hummed the first bar of the title song from *Dog in Pain.*

But Esther did not love Pagan, and she could not desert the Compound. When they walked back down Seventh Avenue, she could not forget the mimosa trees, or her father's eyes, or the cool stone beach at low tide. She stayed with Pagan for the rest of that day, but she had decided to go home.

In the morning when the sun had not yet risen, and Pagan was still asleep, Esther the Black dressed and walked quickly through the living room, where the lead guitarist had fallen asleep on the couch with a tequila bottle still in his hand. She sat in the kitchen and began to write Ira a note; Esther was trying to explain why they weren't meant for each other when the telephone rang.

The evening before, the family had discovered that Esther the Black was not the only missing person in the Compound. Phillip was not at home with Rose, he was not in his recovery cottage, he was not sitting on the lawn or on the stone beach. Cohen had searched for him all night; and, in the morning, when Sam Gardner's bulldozers, which had been parked outside the gate on Route 16 all night, first entered the gate, Cohen suggested to Esther the White that Esther the Black be found. Cohen had believed, from the start, that Esther the Black would be found with Ira Rath—she did not have many friends to choose from. He called Solomon Rath and jotted down Ira's new phone number.

"Esther?" Cohen said, when Esther the Black picked up the receiver. "Esther?" Cohen repeated, though he had not yet heard her voice. Outside, on Tenth Avenue, no buses ran. The city was dark, black as night; but across the river, a pale light glowed above New Jersey.

"What happened?" Esther the Black asked. She knew something was wrong; it was too early, too dark.

"I'm pretty smart," Cohen said. "I figured out where you were." His voice was low; he sounded like an old man.

"Something's happened," Esther said.

"Your father," Cohen said. "Phillip is missing."

Esther the Black ran down the three flights of stairs; she hailed a cab on Twentieth Street; her knuckles were white as the driver sped through the empty morning streets to the pier where the St. Fredrics ferry docked. After she had bought her ticket, Esther waited on the pier for the ferry to board. As the sky turned from gray to summer blue, she tried to distract herself, she tried to think of Ira Rath, but she felt no love, she felt only guilt, for having left him asleep in the dark apartment, dreaming of "Nova Scotia Avenue." She wondered if he seemed to need her so much only because she still called him Ira; but even that was past: he had now become Pagan to her too.

By the time the ferry had boarded and had begun straining its engines, by the time it pulled slowly away from the pier, Esther the Black could no longer avoid it—she looked across the moving water and thought of Phillip. And she found herself wishing, over and over again, that it was not too late; although she knew that for some things, it was always too late. She knew that even if she had been at the Compound the evening before, she could never have stopped Phillip. She might not even have wanted to.

It was a well-known fact that Phillip's drowning attempts happened only once a year, but this year was not like all other years, this year the earth trembled and the pine trees waited to be cut down, one by one. No one could have known that Phillip really would walk down to the sea wall so late in the season, or that he would have the strength to climb it. But his bare feet had held to the sandstone like barnacles. When he reached the beach, Phillip's breathing was heavy; he slipped on the slick green stones and cut the soles of his feet. He would have liked to stop, to wait for a while, not because of the blood which oozed from his feet, but because he would want to look closely at the harbor. But there simply wasn't time. There hadn't been since he had first heard the rumbling.

And so, he walked along the rocks; the sun was strong, his head was light, and behind him he left a thin trail of blood over the algae. It was low tide; the smell of sea lavender and seaweed circled the beach like a fist. Phillip's feet sank into the wet sand; around his toes were the strands of seaweed and the battered shells dropped by high-flying gulls. The centers of his eyes were like fine dark pins, seeing only the horizon, the center where blue meets with blue, where everything joins. Now he knew that everything else had been practice, everything else had been for this one evening in the last week of August.

Before, a part of him had been playing—he had not swum far enough, or not quickly enough, in a river or sea that was slow-moving or warm. Before there had been plenty of time. And he had had a daughter to worry about. But now, Phillip felt that Esther the White would take care of the girl; and now the bulldozers were waiting to push their way through the eastern section of the Compound to the harbor. There was no time.

Phillip stood waist high in water. His pale beige slacks turned to fins, the hair on his legs and genitals was washed away with the cold August tide. And in front of him was the blue where it met with itself, and behind him was the family which still believed that he was just trying to kill himself. Phillip smiled at that thought, as horseshoe crabs moved around him, guarding him like underwater tanks. He breathed as deeply as he could, waves wet his T-shirt until the material stuck to him like a film.

The blue light from the horizon stayed with him, protectively, as Phillip dove deeper; and soon he did not have to dive—he was carried with the tide, around and down. He was carried like a dancer, down like a dancer, with his clear eyes closed. The harbor did not give him up until late the next afternoon, when the current had taken him miles down the beach, and the leg of Phillip's slacks had caught on a wooden piling of the St. Fredrics docks.

Ferries to Manhattan and Connecticut rushed past him, seagulls rested on his knees. Finally he was found by two dock workers who had their lunch each afternoon on the same dock stairs. On the day when Esther the Black arrived back at the Compound the two dock workers shared sandwiches, beer, peaches, and pie; and as they chewed and threw crumbs and pieces of crust into the water, they did not know quite what it was that rolled beneath the dock with calm movements, as elegantly as some huge fish. By the time they realized that it was a man, Phillip's hair was moving in slow curls, and his face was as clear and smooth as a stone.

IV. GATHERING THE NETS

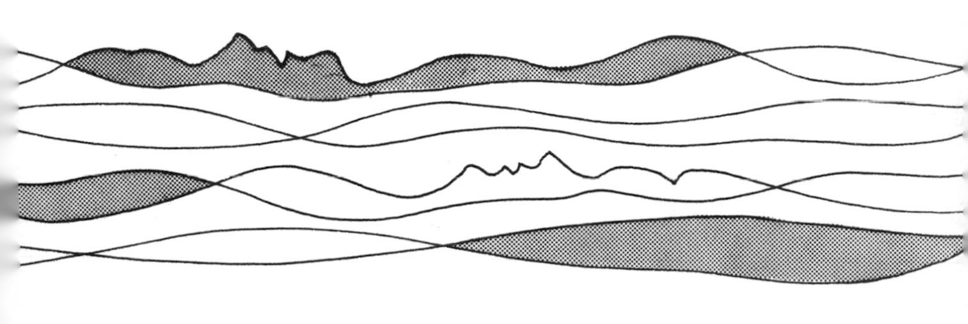

1

They buried him quickly. They had to; Mischa was afraid that the rabbi he had finally persuaded to officiate at Phillip's funeral would discover the possibility of suicide. The spot they chose was as close to the sea wall as the sand would allow; they could hear the bulldozers droning like flies. No one wore black. Mischa leaned on a fine wooden cane, Rose wore a pastel cotton dress, Esther the White's bowed head was draped with pale blue silk, Esther the Black wore sunglasses and her denim cap. From afar, the family appeared to be setting out for a picnic, but two gravediggers leaned on their shovels, and they cursed at the heat and at the fine, sandy earth, which kept refilling the hole they dug.

No one cried; except for Rose, who had been drinking heavily all morning, and who worried about her financial situation as she waved aside the drooping veil of pink chiffon which fell from the brim of her straw hat. Esther the Black did not cry because she could not believe that her father was inside the coffin, which was placed on two wooden boards above the open grave; she imagined that they had found the wrong man. Phillip could not be inside that box; he was somewhere adrift in the waters of the harbor. And if he was in there, Esther the Black thought, then all she had to do was to find a knife and slit the black ribbon which was wrapped like a seal across the coffin's center; then she would see him one more time, she would watch as Phillip sprang forth, surviving yet another drowning.

Esther the White was the only member of the family who had not been at all surprised by Phillip's second drowning in this season; she believed that it was truly her son inside the coffin. Although she had always been sure she would survive him, although she had imagined Phillip's funeral dozens of times, she had not thought that she would be so cold as she stood by the open grave, or so angry that the workmen continued to curse the heat as they dropped the coffin into the earth; she had certainly not thought that she would be so tired that she would be forced to lean on Cohen's arm.

"Esther," Cohen whispered to her as the rabbi began to chant, "how are you doing?"

"Not very well," Esther the White said.

"Are you sick?" Cohen asked.

Esther the White shook her head. "Tired."

Esther the Black could no longer look at the rabbi or the coffin; she stared across the Compound lawn. She wondered if Phillip's death had been her fault; if she had been there the drowning might not have happened. She might have raced across the green stones and thrown her arms around him; he was so light that she could have picked him up and carried him over the sea wall. But Cohen had been there; and the truth was, he was a much better guard than Esther the Black could ever have been. And really, Esther the Black had always known that there was one thing Phillip wanted to do: he wanted to float away, to move with the waves in the middle of the night, through the eelgrass, and the sand, as quietly as any fish, and much, much lighter than air. Esther the Black took off her dark sunglasses, she thought of Phillip moving freely in the waves, she remembered how clear his eyes were; then she saw something begin to cross the Compound lawn. She was the first to see them; slowly, the fishermen were moving across the lawn like a tidal wave. Some were on foot, some drove their old station wagons and vans right over the leveled earth that had once been the pine grove. Esther the Black caught Cohen's eye, she nodded toward the eastern section. The line of fishermen grew nearer; the children and women covered their heads with scarves in the bright sunlight, the men wore caps, their steps shook the earth.

"What is this?" Mischa said, as the fishermen circled the gravesite.

The rabbi looked up and removed his glasses. "Should I continue?" he asked Mischa.

"What is this?" Mischa pointed a finger at several of the old men who drew near him.

The fishermen were silent; their heads were bowed.

"Should I stop the service?" the rabbi asked.

Mischa pounded his cane on the ground. "Out," he said to the crowd. "Get out of here."

"We're here to pay respects to the Drowned Man," the oldest Bolo player said.

"What do you know about respect?" Max said. "You have the nerve to bother my poor brother when his son is under the dirt? I don't believe it."

"Believe it," a young fisherman called out.

"Please," the rabbi said.

"Continue," Esther the White told him.

"How can we continue with these thieves breathing all over me?" Mischa said.

Esther the White had never seen the fishermen at such close range. She knew that Cohen was their friend, she had imagined Cohen sitting in their campground, she had imagined the way the light flashed from their blue headbands as they bent over the fire to lift up the iron coffeepot. When the old Bolo player walked up to Esther the White and stretched out his hand, Esther the White noticed that his hand was like a claw.

"My sympathies," the old fisherman said.

Esther the White took his hand and nodded. She saw no reason why these men, who worked the harbor that her son had loved, should not be there. "Continue," she called loudly to the rabbi.

The rabbi chanted quickly; the odors of gasoline and fish and salt rose in the air. The gravediggers picked up their shovels, they stood at attention; the rabbi cast down the first handful of earth.

"I don't want them to bury him," Esther the White told Cohen. "Those men," she pointed to the gravediggers. "I don't want them to bury him."

Cohen left her side. As he walked over and took a shovel from one gravedigger's hand, Esther the White relaxed. It was right that Cohen should bury him; caring for Phillip had been his job. The earth fell loudly on the wood; gulls circled. No one left the site until the job was done, until Cohen had returned the shovel to the gravedigger, and the rabbi had left.

Rose leaned against the sea wall and wept; the heat and the gin she had drunk earlier flowed through her; she wiped her eyes with her fist and straightened the veil of her straw hat. She was the beneficiary of Phillip's life-insurance policy—but the policy wasn't worth much. Solomon Rath had gotten it from a small company in New Jersey as a favor to the family—so that Mischa could show his son that his suicide attempts were laughable: not even an insurance company would believe them. Rose's pink veil was glued to her face with tears; a widow, standing alone at the sea wall, with nothing to count on but the good graces of her family. And they would be good to her now. Rose smiled. She was a widow, and widows did not sit poolside at the Dunes Hotel, dragging their black veils through chlorine; widows were respected and taken care of by the surviving members of the family.

"Esther," Rose called to her mother-in-law when Esther the White turned from the grave. Rose walked away from the sea wall, glad that they were about to leave the gravesite and get out of the white-hot sun, "Esther, let me help you."

Esther the White stopped; she watched as Rose reached for her arm. "Do I need help?" she said.

"You've had a shock," Rose said, brushing the pink veil from her shoulder.

"What shock?" Esther the White said. "Where have you been that Phillip's drowning is a surprise?"

Rose held Esther the White's arm; she began to lead her to the main house. "Let's get away from the scene of the accident," she whispered, like a widow, like a nun.

The family began to walk toward the main house; the fishermen followed. Mischa bent down and said to his brother, "Wait a minute." He turned to the crowd of silent poachers and cried, "Go away. Go." He waved his hand in the air as if he spoke to bluejays or crows. The family continued on. "You got to treat them like that," Mischa confided to Max.

"But they're still following," Max said.

Mischa faced the fishermen. "What are you following for?" he shouted to the crowd.

Esther the White turned. "Don't yell," she said. "It's bad for you."

Cohen walked with the old Bolo expert. "What's going on?" he said.

The old man shrugged.

"Are you going to hold the family for ransom?" The crowd was crossing the lawn; soon they would be at the porch steps. "You don't even have guns—you're going to hold a bunch of people for ransom on such a hot day without guns? Never work."

"No ransom," the old man said. "No guns. We're just not leaving."

Cohen had not mowed the lawn for a week; pretty soon there would be dandelions if he didn't watch out.

"So what's your plan?" Cohen whispered.

"No plan," the fisherman answered. "Just not leaving."

Cohen patted the Bolo expert on the back. "Nice try," he said. He jogged ahead to catch up with Mischa and Max. "Listen to this," he called out. Mischa waved him away. "Listen, they say they're not leaving."

"Hah," said Mischa.

Cohen shrugged. The family had reached the main house, but the crowd of fishermen and women was still gathered. And when Cohen had stared at them for some time, he realized that the old fisherman hadn't been fooling. The poachers were staying. "They're not kidding," he said to no one, to himself. And then he waved his arms in the air. "You're crazy," he yelled. "Good luck," he told them.

"Cohen," Mischa screamed from the porch stairs. "Cohen, you traitor, shut up and get over here."

"Don't yell," Esther the White told her husband, but she, too, had stopped on the porch to watch the crowd.

The young fisherman, Daniel, raised both his arms in the air; and on that signal, the fishermen began to run. They raced over the Compound lawn, running down the paths, kicking up sand with their feet.

"Call the police," Max said.

"They'll live to regret this," Mischa said. "If the police won't kick them out, I will."

"Why should you care?" Esther the White said. The Compound lawn was moving, alive with bodies, alive with cries. "This place legally belongs to Solomon Rath now. It's his headache. So, what does it matter?"

"It's the moral point, Esther."

Esther the White sighed. Inside her pocket, her fingers stroked the jade pendant she had been waiting to give to her granddaughter; she wished everyone else would go inside and leave them alone. "It doesn't matter if they stay," she said to Mischa.

"It doesn't matter?" Mischa repeated. "Look at them." He pointed his finger. The fishermen were opening the doors of all the houses, the cottage where Phillip had been locked for twenty years of Drowning Seasons, the house which Rose and Phillip shared with Esther the Black in every other season, Max's cottage, the lighthouse, the houses which had never been lived in at all. There was a low, constant murmuring as every house, each room, was examined. Every house except for the main house where Esther the White and Mischa lived. Not one fisherman walked up the steps to that house. When a boy of fourteen was about to open the kitchen window of the main house and climb right through, leaving his footprints on the windowsill, an older man, the boy's father or uncle, grabbed him by his arm and led him away. Esther the Black sat in the wicker rocker and lit a cigarette; she watched as a light was turned on in her own bedroom. The fishermen had climbed the stairs, their children had run their palms over the walls, and now they were opening all the windows; curtains in her bedroom window moved in the night. Esther the Black watched her room, as if it belonged to someone else, and then she turned to the landscape artist, who was hanging on to the porch banister.

"Cohen," she asked. "Do you think they'll stay?"

Children were running across the Compound lawn; station wagons were parked on the paths which would soon be bordered by September roses. Mischa's face was white with anger;

Max was purple with fear. Later in the evening, a few guests would sit shiva for Phillip: the accountant, Rath, who Esther the White found she could be polite to, because it no longer mattered who held the title to the Compound, would cry for his own son, who had deserted him for rock and roll; the builder, Sam Gardner, would drink sweet sherry and pinch the lint from his maroon jacket; Phillip's analyst, Dr. Otto, would already be packing for his winter in Manhattan, and would find the time only to send a telegram.

"Will they really stay?" Esther the Black asked again, just as Max sneaked into the hallway, to call the moving company he had contacted weeks before, when Sam Gardner's signature was still wet on the eastern section's bill of sale. He wanted to get his furniture out before the fishermen wrecked the velvet and the wood; he and Lisa had planned to flee to Miami, and he did not intend to let Phillip's death, or the fishermen's arrival, change his plans.

Cohen lit a match, and then killed the flame between his calloused fingers. He wondered if Esther the White would forget him now—if Mischa would take her away from the fishermen, whisk her off to Manhattan or the south of France. "They'll stay," Cohen nodded. He patted Esther the Black's head lightly. "Why shouldn't they stay? Nobody lives in those houses."

Esther the Black was still on the porch, long after everyone had gone inside. She could hear them pulling up hard-backed chairs in the parlor, she could hear Mischa telephoning the police, she could hear him shouting indignantly about squatters' rights. But after a while, all she could hear were the fishermen. When the Compound grew dark, the windows in every house were lit by electricity or by candles; Esther the Black stared at the darkness and the light, and let Phillip's face move through her memory. Her father would no longer be a captive, shut away from the water, locked in a cottage too dark and too small for any man. He was close enough to the harbor now; he could probably feel the earth move when the tides changed.

Esther the Black had not spoken more than a few sentences to anyone in the family since her return from Manhattan; the only one she might have wanted to talk to then was Phillip, but it was too late—all she could do was stare out toward the harbor and imagine his face. So Esther the Black stayed on, in the dark, listening to the fishermen's songs. Their voices were carried high above the Compound; they floated as far as the sea wall, as far as Phillip's grave. Esther the Black listened carefully to the new sound of the Compound; she listened until that sound was too sweet for any outsider to hear, and then, slowly, she walked inside the only house that remained.

2

The next morning the Compound had grown into a small village; all during the night the fishermen had moved their belongings into the houses; some had set up trailers and tents. They nodded to Esther the Black when she walked by, but that was all. Esther the Black felt her aloneness grow tighter, it grew closer to her heart as she watched the fishermen claim the Compound; early in the day, she walked to town to try to get her old job back.

But after she arrived in the store manager's office, the manager simply looked up and down. "No dice," he told her. "You've proved that you're just not a responsible girl." Esther the Black then began the long walk home, through the midday heat; she had no job, and nowhere to go, she could only follow the road which led straight to the Compound gate. There, on her front porch, Esther the White had been waiting since dawn.

Again and again, Esther the White drew out the jade pendant and ran her fingers over the cool face of the carved woman; as she waited for her granddaughter, she wished that Cohen was with her—for courage. Only for courage. Cohen could act as a mediator; if he were to present Esther the Black with the jade pendant, the girl would be less likely to throw the gift in the dirt—or worse, to walk right past Esther the White's outstretched hand. As that day in the last week of August grew later, as the heat rose, Esther the White realized that she did not want Cohen there just for courage. Mischa had come outside, to drink his coffee in the sunlight and glare at the fishermen, whom the sheriff refused to evict. But when Esther the White finally saw Cohen walk across the lawn toward the main house, she knew whom she wanted with her.

Cohen greeted each fisherman as he passed by them; he tipped his beret as if it were a derby. When he reached the largest cottage, he stopped. Suitcases were piled up on the porch, some of Esther the Black's collection of sea skeletons which lined the railings of all the porches had been knocked down, and now lay scattered in the sand. Lisa ran in and out her front door carrying large cardboard boxes, while a group of Bolo players seated at a table near the upstairs window of the cottage looked down on her. Cohen waved up to the Bolo players and turned to Lisa.

"Mrs.," he said, "what is this? An evacuation?"

Lisa placed her hands on her hips. "You're just standing there? Help me."

Cohen groaned. "Mrs.," he said, "you picked a heat wave to rearrange your furniture. Wait till tomorrow."

Lisa pursed her lips. "Some of us are not so lazy. Some of us can't wait till tomorrow."

Cohen shrugged; Esther the White was waiting for him, he had no time for boxes and furniture.

"Cohen."

"I'm a landscape artist," Cohen explained, "not a mover."

Max came out onto the porch wearing a red and yellow Hawaiian shirt. "Let's go," he said to Cohen. "The moving van will be here before noon. I want all the furniture out on the lawn."

Cohen smiled. "Tell me the truth," he said. "Are you a little upset about your new tenants?" He pointed to the fishermen watching them from the upstairs window.

Max folded his hands in front of his chest. He wanted to leave the Compound quietly, with half the profits from the land sale in his checking account, and without disturbing Mischa. He had decided not to tell Mischa of the move, until all the furniture was safely packed away, and there was less chance for an argument between the two brothers. "Cohen," he said, "you are an employee, and we are in the process of moving to Miami. Now, I'll tell you again—all of the furniture goes out onto the lawn."

Cohen smiled broadly. "Back," he said.

"What?" Max growled.

"Bad back," Cohen explained.

"Lucky for you," Max seethed, "that we're leaving this place. Otherwise, I'd fire you."

Cohen shrugged his shoulders, but he felt cheery as he walked across the lawn. "Good morning," he said to Esther the White. "I just said goodbye," he told Mischa. "Sorry I couldn't help them move the furniture, but when you have a bad back, it's no use trying to lift anything."

"Help who move?" Mischa said. He was dressed in a white linen shirt; he unbuttoned the top button.

"Your brother," Cohen said innocently.

"My brother?" Mischa said.

"Off to Miami," Cohen said. "I wish them well."

Esther the White smiled. "Oh, wonderful," she said. "At last they're leaving."

"That flea," Mischa cried. "He sneaks off the minute I give him a cent, the minute there's some trouble with the poachers."

Mischa left Esther the White and Cohen; he raced across the lawn and stood outside Max's cottage, where he yelled loudly through the open door.

"I thought he knew," Cohen said. "I didn't want to shock him."

"He would have found out sooner or later," Esther the White said.

Cohen sat on the porch steps; Esther the White smiled briefly and looked away. "Esther," Cohen said. But she didn't answer; she wished that she had told Phillip her plans for Esther the Black. "Esther," Cohen said, "have you made a decision?"

Esther the White had hidden the pendant when Mischa came out onto the porch, now she reached for it, and she held the stone in the sunlight. She felt as young as a girl, much younger than when she had first picked up the pendant from between the floorboards.

"Esther, we don't have forever," Cohen sighed.

When Esther the Black had returned from town she avoided the family; she had been sitting on a lawn chair down by the sea wall, but the heat had risen so that it was impossible to stay unprotected in the sun. The fishermen were in possession of all the other houses—so Esther the Black walked toward her grandparents' house.

"She's coming this way," Esther the White said when she saw her granddaughter. "Stay with me," she said to Cohen. She felt a twitch beneath her left eye. "Please," she said to Cohen.

Cohen shook his head. "You have to give me an answer."

"Stay with me," Esther the White said.

"You'll have to tell Mischa that you're through with him," Cohen said. "He's a sensible man—he'll understand. Of course I wouldn't want to leave the Compound—but if it's too uncomfortable for you to see Mischa after you leave him, we'll just have to think of another place to live. Maybe out east farther," Cohen said. "I'm not too old to get another job."

"She's here," Esther the White said. "Call her over. I have the jade."

"No," Cohen said. "You call her."

Esther the Black noticed her grandmother on the porch, she noticed Cohen on the stair. They'll both get sunstroke, she thought. Two more funerals.

Esther the White waved her hand in the air. "Esther," she called.

Esther the Black stopped. A fly buzzed across her cheek. The air was so heavy that it seemed to sing. Flies and crickets cried above the heat's constant pitch; the Compound was alive with wings.

"Esther," her grandmother was calling louder now. "Come over here. Over here."

Esther the Black thought of running; she couldn't imagine what her grandmother could want. Could it be to ask where Esther the Black had been, where she had disappeared to; to demand an explanation for the abandoned Cadillac now that the shock of Phillip's death was over? But Cohen was smiling at her, and Esther the Black was thirsty and hot; she walked over and leaned against the banister. She couldn't really be threatened anymore, they couldn't send Phillip anywhere now. Cohen looked at Esther the White. "Well?" he said. "Esther, are you going to talk?"

"Esther?" said Esther the Black, surprised that Cohen would call her grandmother by her first name, wondering if the slip had occurred because the landscape artist sat in the noon sun without protection against the heat.

Esther the White reached out her hand. "Take it," she said.

Esther the Black looked blank; she saw only an old woman's veined hand. "Take what?" she asked.

Esther the White grabbed her granddaughter's hand; she let go of the jade, and the pendant rolled like an egg into the girl's fingers. The sweat from Esther the White's fingers covered the stone with a fine film, and the jade rested in Esther the Black's palm like a living thing.

Esther the Black looked up. "What is this?" she said, wondering if mirages could be cast by the extreme heat—by eleven o'clock the temperature had reached ninety-eight. She needed a glass of water, a Pepsi, or an orangeade. She might have been hallucinating—it would not have been surprising.

"Go ahead," Cohen urged Esther the White.

"Ssh," said Esther the White. She touched Cohen's hand lightly.

Esther the Black stared at the woman carved into the jade. The high cheekbones, the downcast eyes. A river of heat moved between Esther the Black and that woman's face.

Esther the White cleared her throat. From the corner of her eye she could see Mischa shouting at his brother in the heat. "The other day," she began, "before his death, your father reminded me that I never give anything. I wanted to give you something. It was Phillip's suggestion, and it was a good one."

Esther the Black was silent. She had not imagined that her father ever spoke to Esther the White. Cohen poked her shoulder. "Well?" he said proudly. "What do you say?"

"What if I wanted to give this to the fishermen?" Esther the Black said.

Esther the White shrugged. "Do whatever you want. The pendant is yours. But the fishermen are doing fine without your help."

Esther the Black narrowed her eyes. In her head the heat raced, the lyrics to "Nova Scotia Avenue" moved, the odor of honeysuckle reared up. "I can do anything with it?" she asked.

"It's yours," Esther the White answered. "Anything."

"Why?" Esther the Black asked. "You never gave me anything before." She wondered if the pendant had really been Phillip's; he had willed it to her, and Esther the White might be taking the credit.

"I have nothing more to say," Esther the White whispered. "It's just a gift."

"And what do you want from me?" Esther the Black narrowed her eyes. "What's the price?"

"Now, now," Cohen said, looking from one Esther to the other.

Esther the Black's head was reeling; the odors and the noises of the Compound were too strong, they were rocking inside her head. "Do you have anything to drink?" she asked. "A Pepsi?"

Cohen patted his stomach. "Hot drinks are better in hot weather," he said. "They don't shock the system as much. Have some tea."

"All right. Anything." The pendant in her hand was like a piece of carved ice; Esther the Black touched the stone to her forehead.

"You two stay, I'll put the water on. Esther, what kind of tea do you have?" Cohen asked.

"Jasmine, orange, peppermint," Esther the White answered.

"Peppermint," Cohen nodded. "Wonderful."

Esther the Black's eyes were wide; her grandmother was smiling at the landscape artist. "How is it," Esther the Black turned to Cohen, "that you suddenly call my grandmother by her first name?"

"What makes you think it's sudden?" Cohen said. "Maybe it's only sudden to you."

Esther the Black closed her eyes. She wondered how many people had recently died of thirst, and if the statistics were stored in the St. Fredrics town hall. Still, she hoped that Cohen would not leave her alone with Esther the White, not even if she did die of thirst.

Esther the White stared over at the Compound gate. "It is true," she said. "They're leaving for Miami."

A large blue and white van edged through the gate. Cohen slapped his knee. "Good riddance," he said.

"Bad rubbish," Esther the White agreed.

"Who else leaves a sinking ship but rats?" Cohen said, as Mischa followed Max and Lisa, shouting and waving his fist

"If you consider this a sinking ship," Esther the White added.

Esther the Black looked at her grandmother. She looked at Cohen. She felt like a foreigner, a deaf-mute, a stranger. She ran her tongue over her parched lips. "You two," she addressed herself to Cohen. "What's between you two?"

Cohen was proud of her; he patted Esther the Black's shoulder. If he considered the situation, he would have to say that the girl had been raised under his influence—and she certainly wasn't stupid. "Your grandmother and I have settled things."

"Things?" Esther the Black said. "What things?"

Cohen waved his hand in the air. "Things you don't know about. You're too young to know about such things."

"Let's eavesdrop," Esther the White said to Cohen. "I want to be certain that Max is really leaving. I never really trusted him. Not one bit."

The moving men had begun to load the van with furniture. Mischa declared that every piece belonged to him.

"Don't touch that chair," Mischa held on to gold brocade.

"Half of everything is mine," Max shouted.

Up on the porch, Esther the White breathed deeply; she

had always considered Lisa and Max to be intruders; it was a good omen that they would finally be gone.

"Just watch," Cohen whispered to Esther the White, as he stroked the sleeve of her blouse. "Watch them tear that chair in half."

Esther the Black no longer had the strength to be puzzled; she sat on the porch steps as if it were a natural thing to watch Cohen and her grandmother touching, as if it were common to be given a huge jade and gold pendant. But every now and then, when Esther the White laughed, or when Cohen made a sudden noise scratching a wooden match along his boot heel, Esther the Black turned her head like a bird, nervously, expecting anything at all to happen.

"They shouldn't argue so much," Esther the White said after a while, when the moving van was nearly loaded, and the brothers continued to scream and accuse. "It's too hot. They're too old."

As she spoke Mischa turned and stared across the lawn, as if somehow he could have heard her. He placed a hand to his chest. "Heart," he said.

"What did he say? What is he doing?" Cohen cried, as Esther the White quickly rose.

"It's his heart," Esther the White said.

Mischa's posture was crazily bent, but Max seemed not to notice—he continued ordering moving men to lift the velvet couch more carefully. Esther the White ran across the lawn in the strongest heat of the day.

"Oh, shit," Cohen said. "Shit."

Esther the Black was convinced that everything around her was disappearing into the heat; everything except for the cool jade pendant she held in her hand. The moving men were carrying Mischa back to the main house; as they passed Esther the Black on the porch steps, she noticed that her grandfather was surrounded by a horde of lazy, buzzing flies.

"We've got to call a doctor," Esther the White said, as she followed Mischa and the movers into the house.

Cohen and Esther the Black listened to the echo of the slamming screen door. It was impossible to see inside the dark hallway, even when they shaded their sun-strained eyes. Max and Lisa stood at the bottom of the steps. Max shook his head. "Disasters," he said. "One disaster right after another. If he dies, it's because of me."

"Please," Cohen said. "He's not dead so quick."

Esther the Black slipped the jade pendant into the front pocket of her jeans; she walked into her grandparents' house. In the hallway, Esther the White was describing symptoms over the telephone, and Mischa lay on a dark green rug in the parlor, with the moving men standing around him. Esther the Black walked through the cool, dark house; her head was light, her feet seemed to rise above the wood. In the kitchen, Esther the Black leaned against the opened refrigerator and drank from a green glass bottle of lemonade. She could hear the conversation on the porch through an open window: Rose had joined the others, and she began to ask questions, as if she had been sent to the Compound by a detective agency. Flies were buzzing over a teacup where a slice of lemon had been left to dry.

Outside, the fishermen were hanging up nets to dry in the afternoon sun, seagulls sat in circles on the lawn, and it was summer, even though August was disappearing and Drowning Season was finished. Because nothing would ever be the same again, Esther the Black stayed in the kitchen alone. She sat at the wooden table and drank lemonade; she drank when she wasn't even thirsty anymore; and still, when the kitchen was dark and the moon was rising over the harbor, Esther the Black held the jade pendant in the palm of her hand, knowing that nothing would ever be the same again, and wishing that she could stay just a little while longer.

3

Mischa recovered. The only traces of his renegade heart were a very slight paralysis on his left side and a desire for warm weather. Max demanded total responsibility for Mischa's attack; and he stayed on after Lisa and the movers had left for Miami. He sat at his brother's feet and told circus stories and warned against smoking cigars; and after a while he convinced Mischa that the best remedy for an ailing heart was the aqua blue sky of Miami.

Mischa assumed that Esther the White would follow his fragile heart to Miami, but Esther the White had never thought of living anywhere but the Compound.

"Listen to me, Esther," Mischa said, and he spoke softly

because Max sat on a feathered quilt at his bedside. "I'm a sick man, and I need the sun."

Esther the White considered telling Mischa about her own illness; right then the pain was moving along her side like a snake. "Florida," she said. "I never thought of going to Florida."

"Think about going," Mischa said. "Just think about it. We've been together for a long time."

Esther the White smiled. Not just a long time; they had been together forever. And what did she have in the Compound—a granddaughter who refused to love her, an old landscape artist who wanted her to pretend she was young, and a son buried near to the sea wall. "Miami." Esther the White shrugged.

"Take my advice," Max said. He crossed his legs and exhaled cigar smoke. "You're better off without her. I can take care of you."

Esther the White went to the window. The bulldozers had been working for nearly two days; now and then the house moved, as if some small underground earthquakes shook up the sand.

"I might go," Esther the White said, as the bulldozers chased bluejays from the mimosas in the eastern section. "I will go," she finally said.

As Mischa, Max, and Esther the White prepared to leave for Miami, the family lived together under one roof for the first time. Max and Mischa shared a bed, as they had done when they were children. Rose threw down pillows and quilts on the parlor floor for herself and Esther the Black. Cohen and Esther the White sat in the kitchen each night, drinking hot tea with lemon and waiting for the rest of the family to go to their rooms. And then, as Max packed trucks full of Mischa's suits and shirts, Cohen would shake the covers on the cot that had been set up for him in the pantry. When Rose closed her eyes and pulled a sheet around herself, Cohen washed the teacups and Esther the White dried the cups with a blue-and-white checkered cloth. And by the time Esther the Black was turning in her sleep, dreaming of her father's soft drowned eyes or of Pagan Rath's offers and promises, Esther the White and Cohen had already walked up the stairs to the large bedroom on the left.

Esther the White's suitcases were already packed. "I have to go to Miami," she told Cohen one night. "I owe it to Mischa; we've spent our lives together."

Cohen sat on the bed. "You'd be miserable, Esther," he said. "The sun down there would drive you crazy. You've been together with Mischa too long; you've forgotten what you want to do."

They had slept together for several nights, Esther had even turned off the lamp, but they had not yet made love. "We're too old," Esther the White had said each night, as they lay together under blue sheets, listening to the night cries of the fishermen rowing out into the harbor. "We'll make noise," Esther now told Cohen, and she pushed his hand away when he tried to touch her. She planned to leave the next morning for Florida with Mischa and Max; there was no point in Cohen's touching her now—it was too late. But when he reached for her again, later that night, Esther the White could think of nothing she wanted more than Cohen's arm around her waist.

"Listen," Cohen said, finally, "at least let me put a light back on. Let me see you."

"What's to see?" Esther the White said.

"Everything. You."

"Whisper," Esther the White said.

"For what?" Cohen lit a cigarette.

Esther the White blinked like an owl when Cohen switched on the lamp. She nodded her head to the wall. "Mischa might hear," she said. "I don't want him to know about this affair."

"Is this an affair?"

"Are you in my bed?"

"No one will hear," Cohen said. "We don't have to be so quiet."

"I'm old. I think I forgot how." Cohen's hand was touching her leg. Esther the White swallowed; she didn't want him to touch her, she didn't want him not to touch her. She thought now that sleeping alone was like an addictive poison. "I think I forgot," she repeated; but Cohen was not listening, his pulse was too loud to hear Esther's whispering voice, until she asked: "And what makes you think you can still do it?"

Cohen moved his hand from her skin, and reached to the night table to put out his cigarette. "Still fuck?" Cohen asked.

Esther the White felt like a traitor in the dark; the blue sheets were cold, the beginnings of her pain moved like ice. She didn't answer him.

"Are you shocked by what I said?" Cohen asked.

"Not at all."

Cohen shook his head. "Too bad. I wanted to shock you."

Esther the White laughed. Cohen was insulted.

"It's funny?" he said. "It's not funny, Esther. What are we, twenty years old? It just may surprise you to know that I can still get it up."

"Oh," said Esther the White.

"Not so often, of course," Cohen said. "But, I haven't forgotten. And I can only say, you're not with the times. Nowadays it's a recognized fact that fucking isn't the only thing. That's right. Especially for women."

Esther the White was embarrassed; she had been married for more than forty years, she had had lovers—but she had slept alone for as long as she had lived in the Compound, for as long as a lifetime, and she didn't know any new facts. "So," she said, "what are you? An expert?"

"I read," Cohen shrugged.

Esther the White stiffened; she told Cohen to be quiet because she had heard something. Downstairs, on the parlor floor, Esther the Black was dreaming. In her dream, Pagan Rath had turned a yellow Volkswagen onto a Pacific cliff; beyond was the ocean, and high black rocks. In her dream, Esther the Black reached out, but she only succeeded in knocking over a potted palm onto the floor. In the parlor, a terra cotta pot shattered. Rose's sleepy voice drifted upstairs.

Up in the bedroom, Cohen sighed. "Nothing's changed," he said. "What's the difference if I talk to you across the bed, or across the kitchen table."

Esther the White was silent; she wished she could cry, but the sadness never seemed to reach her eyes—it stuck in her throat, unable to be moved. "I'm sorry," she said.

Cohen lit another cigarette, his hands shook. Dummy, he said to himself. After waiting all these years to get close to her, what do you do but argue? Argue when you should kiss. "No," he told Esther the White. "Don't be sorry, I'll be sorry. There's nothing that could make me sorrier than you leaving for Miami. Nothing could make me sorrier than if you turn away now," he whispered.

Esther the White concentrated. Slowly, as Cohen smoked his cigarette, as the moon grew higher, and the frogs began to call at the sea wall, she remembered other lovers. She remembered Mischa, when he was young, when he was her lover—how he seemed afraid of a kiss, how she often had to reach for him and place him inside of her; how both Mischa and Esther the White felt they were being watched in the act of love—first by the horses behind the blankets in the stable in Marseilles, and later by memories of the village of their childhood, of their parents, of Max as he stood beside the circus manager, his dark eyes wet and accusing. She thought of the taxi driver in London; she had to think for a while before she could remember his name; but she did remember his touch. And she wondered now, as she held on to the blue sheets, if she had ever known how to love.

Esther asked Cohen for a cigarette; she leaned back and

rested her head on two feather pillows, and remembered the tattooed man, Solo.

They had stood in the cold, dark rooming house in Marseilles, and beneath his shirt were the colors of his wonderful tattoos, like some painted secret moving in the dark. For such a very long time she had tried not to imagine Solo; it took quite a while before she could picture the talons of the parrot which rode on his skin. She had known him for only weeks, but had hated him for a lifetime. It was the tattooed man Esther cursed at the moment Phillip was born; it was his name—Solo—she screamed when she first dug in the Compound earth to bury the earrings along with the jade pendant—the stone she might have sold, the stone that might have kept Max from the circus, and Esther the White from taking the tattooed man as her first lover. Phillip might have been his child; Esther the White might have gone off with him to Spain, if only the tattooed man had asked. And so, many years later, Esther still remembered the tattoos as if they had been etched onto her own skin just from their touching. As if she had caught something.

With him she had given everything up, she had let go, for a moment. With the tattooed man she forgot standing in the snow in the village, wandering over the ice to stare at her face in the river; she forgot slipping the jade pendant into her apron pocket. Maybe it was only the way he moved inside of her, maybe it was because it was the first time, or because she saw a vision of his tattoos when she closed her eyes, but Esther the White had felt something. And between cold sheets, as the frogs called, and the bulldozers drove through the dark morning, Esther the White remembered. She reached out for Cohen and remembered.

Later that morning, Max and Mischa finished their packing. When Mischa looked at his empty closet on the morning he was to leave the Compound, his suits and shirts and winter coats were now being carefully moved by Railway Express, he let his cane drop to the floor; and while Max waited on the porch for the limousine which would take the brothers to the airport, Mischa dragged a wooden chair into the closet, and there he sat, beneath one unlit bulb. The cord of the lightbulb danced across his forehead, and he brushed it away, as if he were waving off flies. He worried about the poachers, he worried about Solomon Rath, he could not imagine the hot sun of Miami no matter how hard he tried. He lit a cigar; after a while the ash fell onto his pants leg. The houses in the Compound were abandoned, the poachers were official squatters. What could he do? He was tired; he considered himself a dead man. In fact Mischa would not die for some time; he would not have a final heart attack for years, and then it would be after eating blueberry pancakes in Junior's, as two elderly women from Detroit affectionately watched his teeth turn purple with berries. But on that morning, Mischa brushed the light cord away, and sighed. When he heard his brother call out that the limousine had arrived, Mischa went to the open window and looked down.

"A minute," he said. He picked up his cane and walked down the hall. "Esther," he said, tapping against the door. "It's me."

"It's Mischa," Esther the White whispered. Cohen was still asleep, so Esther the White left the bed and dressed quickly. She went out into the hallway and closed the door behind her. "Mischa," she said, "it's so early."

"You're not ready?" Mischa asked. They stood in the hallway like strangers. "When we left our village together you were ready first, it was your idea, you'll remember. I, personally, never thought we'd make it through the ice."

Esther the White hooked her arm through Mischa's and helped him down the stairs. The entrance hallway was littered with suitcases; Esther the Black and Rose waited solemnly at the door. Rose held a drink in her hand.

"Well, we have this house," Rose whispered to Esther the

Black. "We should be thankful for that. We should be thankful that your grandparents didn't kick us out on the street the day after your father died." She sipped gin. "But I'll be damned if I'm staying here." She looked around at the hallway and the parlor nervously. "Not here," she said. "I'll sell off all the furniture, all the silver—they'll never know." She gestured with her head toward Mischa and Esther the White as they walked together down the stairs. "I'll sell off everything, and then you'll see how quick I'm out of here. I'll be on the first plane to Las Vegas."

Esther the Black nodded, but she did not listen to a word her mother said. She had the jade pendant and the money it would bring—she was free to leave the Compound—but she no longer had to flee—the Compound was falling away, the fishermen had it now, the light which always shone from Esther the White's bedroom would be gone. The sea wall itself would probably be washed away before long; and Esther the Black wondered if she would be the only one to see the sandstone fall away in large, uneven blocks.

At the edge of the stairs, Esther the White stopped. Her granddaughter was huddled in a corner of the hallway, her back against the wall. Esther the White was certain that the girl would be taken care of—Mischa would send allowance checks from Miami, and Esther the White would continue writing monthly checks to the electric company and the fuel company. And the girl had the jade pendant—she was free to make her own decisions. She was old enough, and free. Still, she looked too young standing in the hallway, edged up against the wall. Esther the White turned to Mischa; he looked like an old man, like a stranger; upstairs the man she loved turned in his sleep, and when he reached out he touched only air.

"I'm not going," Esther the White said.

Esther the Black looked up; Rose spilled a bit of gin on her blouse.

"Of course you are," Mischa said.

Esther the White shook her head. "Sorry," she said. "I can't."

The movers came for the suitcases in the hallway, and Esther the White asked them to leave hers behind. "I don't want to," she told Mischa.

Max stuck his head in the door. "Time," he said. "It's time."

"We've been together a long time," Esther the White said to Mischa. "We've been together forever. But now I want to stay, and Max will take care of you."

"I'm going to get a condominium right near Max's place. You'll like it," Mischa said, wondering why the woman he spoke to looked nothing like the girl from his village, the girl he had married.

"Max will take good care of you," Esther the White repeated.

Rose's eyes lit up; she placed her drink on the telephone table. "Max doesn't know how to take care of a sick man," she said. "Taking care of a sick man is an art." She reached for her purse, which rested on the telephone table, next to the glass of gin; she adjusted the shoulder strap and smiled. "You don't have anything to worry about," she told Mischa. "I'll take care of you," she said.

"Oh, no," Mischa said. "I couldn't ask you to do that."

"Nonsense," Rose said. She turned to Esther the Black. "Darling, you can pack up my clothes and mail them down to me. Until I get them I can just pick up a few things in Miami. Little blouses and bermuda shorts—I really don't have the wardrobe for the kind of heat they have down there." She smiled.

"Mother," Esther the Black said. "What about Nevada?"

"Oh, Esther," Rose said, "one hot climate is the same as another."

"Let her go," Esther the White said to Mischa. "You won't be alone. And let's face it," she lowered her voice, "we haven't shared a room for years."

Mischa swallowed; all his suitcases were packed. "You're sure?" he said to Esther. And when she nodded, he shook his head. "I have to go," Mischa said. "Max is waiting for me."

"Of course," Esther the White agreed, and she walked with him to the doorway. Rose ran out to the limousine Max had ordered to drive them to the airport. "Miami should be lovely this time of year," Esther the White said. "Hot." Mischa nodded, and when he turned to say goodbye Esther the White kissed his lips and patted his shoulder. Esther the White watched as Max and Rose helped Mischa into the limousine; she stood at the door until the limousine had disappeared through the iron Compound gate.

Esther the Black had not moved. Her heart hurt; she had begun to dream each night of rescuing people who refused to be rescued.

"So," Esther the White said, after she had closed the front door, "what do you do now?"

"Could I have some privacy?" Esther the Black said coldly. "I'd like to make a phone call."

Esther the White wanted to tell her granddaughter not to slouch; she wanted to say, Don't be a fool, sell the jade pendant and you'll have enough money to do whatever you like. She wanted to tell Esther the Black that if an old woman could make love in the gray morning beneath blue sheets, a young one like Esther the Black could do anything she wanted.

Esther the Black dialed Pagan Rath's number. She did not know what she would do now; but she knew that she did not love Pagan—she could not go with him to California.

"We could help each other," Esther the White began to call from the stairs; but when she reached the landing she could no longer speak. She had to stop. Her hand was on the banister, her granddaughter stared rudely from the hallway, and Esther the White held a fist to her ribs.

"Do you mind?" Esther the Black called, as she held her hand over the phone receiver.

"Not at all," Esther the White said. "Everyone's entitled to privacy." She forced her feet upstairs; each time she moved her legs the pain shot across her abdomen. When she reached her room, she wished that Cohen had somehow disappeared. But he hadn't; he was still in bed smoking a cigarette and dropping ashes on the sheets. "You didn't go with him," Cohen said. "I knew you couldn't."

"Of course I didn't go," Esther the White said. "What made you think I would?"

Cohen reached out for her from the bed, but Esther the White ignored him. She walked to her night table, and searched for her pill bottle. Maybe they're not here, she thought. Maybe the bluejays came through the open window and picked out the Demerol. She threw bottles of aspirin and Darvon onto the rug.

"Esther?" Cohen said.

It's a punishment, Esther the White thought. It's a punishment for not going to Miami, for thinking of myself. So now I'm getting this; now they're giving me the pain.

Cohen sat up. "What is it?" he said.

Esther the White found the Demerol; she dropped the pill on her tongue and swallowed. She sat on the edge of the bed and rocked back and forth. Cohen moved toward her and touched her shoulder. Only a few minutes, Esther the White thought. Soon the Demerol will take over; I can wait till then. Cohen was holding her by the time the medication had begun to wipe out the pain; Esther the White lay back and imagined that she was covered by the quilts of her childhood, heavy red and white cotton filled high with goose feathers.

"I want you to call that doctor," Cohen said. "I think you

should go to the hospital, even though I know you don't believe in anything modern."

Esther the White pulled herself out of the ice, so that she could answer him. "Modern?" she said. "What's modern about death? Everyone knows once you go into the hospital you don't come out."

Cohen was insistent; Esther wanted him to shut up, she wanted him to hold her and let her fall asleep between the blue sheets and the heavy quilts whose geese had once run across the frozen river of her childhood. "Just as an outpatient," Cohen was saying, as the geese dropped their thick white feathers onto the ice. "You'll never have to sleep in the hospital. I'll wait for you in the parking lot, you'll sleep with me every night. Just go for treatments."

Esther the White was falling asleep; she shook her head no.

"Listen," Cohen said, "don't decide to die." The sun was falling through the open window as if reflected by drifts of bright snow. "And, anyway," he said, "why don't you wait around to see what Esther the Black does when she sells the pendant?"

Esther the White imagined that nameless woman's carved face, the cheekbones of polished jade, the unnamed eyes gazing carelessly from the stone. And as she did, Esther the Black hung up the phone in the downstairs hallway after talking to Pagan Rath, after giving her regrets; she walked into the parlor, sat in a cushioned chair, and stared at that same carved face beneath a sixty-watt bulb.

"Esther the Black?" Esther the White said. "She doesn't care about me or the pendant. She doesn't even know me."

"Give her a chance," Cohen said. "Do you want to die and still be a stranger to her?"

"You're right," Esther said softly. "As usual." She thought for a minute. "I want to make certain that she does whatever she wants with the jade pendant. I want to tell her how I first got it. She should know something; she should know me. Cohen," Esther the White's voice rose, "tell her I want to talk to her. I have to."

"Only if you make me a promise," Cohen said. He was not about to lose her now.

Esther the White was hearing the wolves; they howled when she was beneath the deep quilts, when the fire in the kitchen burned to ash.

"Promise," Cohen said, "you'll go to the hospital."

Esther the White closed her eyes and ran her fingers across the veins which lined Cohen's wrists. "I'll think about it," she said. "I will." Outside the day was white with the last of summer's heat, outside the bluejays in the mimosa grove called, and the wolves they said lived above, in the mountains, howled; and Esther the White lay back on two feather pillows and thought about Cohen's kisses.

4

They sat together in the dark. Fishermen on their way to the night harbor passed them and nodded. Esther the Black swung her legs nervously. She had promised Cohen she would meet with her grandmother, but neither of them spoke. Esther the White had just awakened from the deep sleep her dosage of Demerol brought on; her clear eyes were clouded in the night, and, if she listened very carefully, she could almost hear the breathing of the horses who had lived on the other side of the heavy wool blanket in the stable she and the brothers had shared in France.

They were sitting by the black sea wall, listening to the slow-moving tide, and the scratching of the scuttling hermit crabs. The voices of the fishermen rowing slowly out on a night's work echoed from the harbor. Esther the White's scarf moved softly, like feathers around her face; she felt no pain. Instead she drifted—in the haze her painkillers offered—from one time to another, one memory to the next. Yet she always came back to the sea wall where she sat in the damp evening air with her granddaughter. She always remembered that she was there to talk to Esther the Black.

"I could never sleep at night," Esther the White said.

"I know," Esther the Black said. "I used to see your light at night. I saw it for years."

"Oh," Esther the White said. "I didn't think anyone noticed." Her granddaughter was silent. "Now I shut the light off. I sleep well at night for the first time. A little bit because of Cohen. A little bit because of the drugs that I have to take now that I'm sick."

Esther the Black stared at her grandmother's half-closed pale eyes; the old woman's blue scarf fell over her forehead. Esther the Black wanted to know why her grandmother kept her here in the dark now that she had talked about her illness. There was something more, and Esther the Black was curious. And she was also afraid—the old woman might want something. There was no one else left—perhaps Esther the White only wanted pity because she was ill. Or maybe the return of the jade pendant, which Esther the Black planned to sell as soon as possible, now that she had told Pagan that she would not fly to Los Angeles with The Quick and the Mad. Pagan Rath had promised that Esther the Black's name would be listed as a guest at the desk of the Normandy Hotel, so that she could join him whenever she decided that she loved him. And she would, Pagan had insisted, decide just that.

"I've written a song for you," he had told Esther the Black when she telephoned him.

"How does it go?" she had asked.

"Come to Los Angeles and you'll hear it," Pagan said.

"No," Esther said.

"Well, you'll hear it on the radio all the time as soon as we record it, and every time you'll think of me."

"Pagan," Esther said, "I never listen to the radio."

He sighed. "Esther the Black, on the day you come back, we'll fly down the alleyways on the wings that I promised you, like we used to do so long ago."

"We never flew down alleyways," Esther interrupted. "You never promised me wings."

"Oh, Esther," Pagan Rath said, "it's only a song. It's poetry. What do you want?"

"I'll let you know where I am," Esther the Black said.

"Do you have the telephone number of the hotel in L.A. in case you change your mind?" Pagan said mournfully.

"Yes," Esther said. "Just in case," she smiled.

The Quick and the Mad were now flying in the night toward Los Angeles. Each time a jet passed over the harbor, Esther the Black looked up; as she sat with her grandmother in the dark, Pagan Rath was drinking a tall glass of Dewar's in the first-class section of an American Airlines 727 jet. Esther the Black imagined herself in the first-class cabin, drinking a Tequila Sunrise with the headphones screwed into her ears, and Pagan staring at her with his soft, watery eyes. She laughed out loud, and breathed in the night air.

"Tell me, tell me," Esther the White now asked her, in a soft, slurred voice, "exactly how old are you?" She was remembering their Notting Hill flat. "How old?" she said.

Esther the Black sighed. "I told you, eighteen."

"That's all," Esther the White mused. "That isn't so much."

A group of fishermen had gathered in the center of the Compound lawn. They raised their fishing nets in the air, and walked down to the harbor.

"They keep the Compound alive," Esther the White said, nodding. She ran her fingers over a rough block of sandstone.

"Maybe the reason I sleep well at night now is that I hear their voices." She turned again to Esther the Black. "I asked you before how old you were because my memory tricks me, I get confused, and I don't want to be confused."

Salt air stuck to Esther the Black's eyelashes; she remembered Esther the White staring at her when she was a child, she stared right through her, with eyes like ice.

"Why are you so interested, all of a sudden?" Esther the Black demanded. "Just because you're sick you think everything's changed? You have cancer, so am I supposed to erase my memory?" She remembered Esther the White standing on the porch, in a Drowning Season long before. Esther the Black wanted to know where Cohen was; she was ten, and there was no one to talk to. Esther the White might not have heard her; she didn't answer, she looked out at the wide cool lawn and ignored her granddaughter. "Why didn't you talk to me then?" Esther the Black said.

They sat together like stone, women carved into the sea wall. Esther the Black remembered kneeling on the dark earth as Rose planted sunflower seeds. Esther the White walked past, not speaking, not looking. Esther the Black watched her grandmother's pale hair move in the wind.

"Don't look at her," Rose had warned.

Esther the Black watched as the earth was turned. "Why not?"

"Don't look at her, and don't bother your grandmother."

Esther the Black watched her mother's hand toss seeds, in a row, into the dark, moving earth. And as they walked on, the bluejays followed like vultures.

"What do you think?" Esther the Black lit a cigarette, and the match sizzled. "You give me one gift, and everything else doesn't count? Every other memory of you is wiped away?"

Esther the White watched her granddaughter: her face was as smooth as sculpture.

"I don't know why we're sitting here. You have nothing to do with my life. I don't even remember you," Esther the Black lied.

Esther the White felt feathers in her throat. Perhaps it was only from the medication, some side effect—but it seemed as if she had swallowed a dove, a pigeon, or a hawk.

"Esther," she said to her granddaughter.

But Esther the Black shrugged. "You're not in my life."

The feathers were rising up in Esther the White's throat, covering her tongue with soft down. "Then I will be," Esther the White said.

"No," Esther the Black insisted, as she listened to the cries of the fishermen from the harbor. "Let's go back to the house," Esther the Black said. She did not want to know her grandmother. She was afraid to.

But it was too late for Esther the Black to turn away; Esther the White had already begun. She had begun with Cohen and with Phillip, and now with Esther the Black. Esther the White did not move an inch; it was as if the stone had been torn apart, and within it was a bird whose feathers were drifting upward. Bits of stone lodged in her organs and in her skin; all across her ribs, there was a thin metallic line of pain. And as the stone shattered, the pain flew upward. She tried to keep her balance on the sea wall, she listened when her granddaughter insisted that they leave, but Esther the White had begun to cry.

At first it was only like something caught in her throat, or like the sharp harbor air. Esther the White was confused, uncertain as to what language to speak in. She tried German, but the words escaped her. She tried French, and then English, but all the sounds ran together, a low howling noise was all that she could make, not words at all. Esther the White did not realize that she was crying, until her granddaughter wiped away the wetness on her face with one hand. Esther the White licked her lips; saltier than ocean water.

"Grandmother, stop it," Esther the Black whispered. "You don't have to do this."

The girl knelt before her in the sand; Esther the White smiled uncertainly at her, but it was too late, it had already begun: Esther the White was planning her escape from her parents' house, the jade pendant sewn into her coat. She had already asked one of the loggers in the village how it would be possible to get away from the village now that the river had frozen and rafts from the village were stuck in yards of ice.

Time shattered slowly inside her, and she traveled in the direction the logger pointed out, over the border, sleeping in the frozen cars of the train; through France with the jade stone in her coat. She tolerated Max, and she dragged Mischa behind her, so that he would not give up and fall into the ice, so that he would not fall back into the village of their childhood. She had decided not to feel anything, and certainly, she had decided that she, herself, would never fall into the ice. Time was shattering like a mirror, and Esther the White remembered how her own eyes changed, how they turned a paler and paler blue, how her skin grew whiter, until she had to cover her head in the sun. She moved through men, watching their eyes change too, from desire to dust, and now, with Cohen, back again to desire. She passed by her own son. Even though strange cells were multiplying in her body, and the pain growing worse, she passed by her own son. She dreamed of a Compound—she invented it, she created a home, and when she spoke, in the darkness, the earth of this Compound rose, sand was carried in the air as she spoke.

"And even now," Esther the White said, "I'll tell you another secret. I've waited all my life, watching the night, trying not to be afraid of the dark, and even now, I'm still afraid, because I think I may die before anyone knows me."

They spoke almost in unison; Esther the Black tried to comfort her grandmother, Esther the White sometimes forgot words and made only the soft howling noise.

"Listen," Esther the Black said, as she tried to find a way to quiet Esther the White, to calm her down. "I want you to be quiet. You be quiet and I'll talk. I'm going to describe the Compound."

Now that Esther the Black realized just how much the Compound meant to her grandmother, she knew just what to say. Esther the Black counted off the lilac, and the wisteria, the purple rose of sharon and the tulips, as if the flowers were a lullabye. Next to her, she felt her grandmother's shivering lessen, the howling grew softer and softer. Esther the White rocked on the sea wall, threads from her skirt caught on the stone. Esther the Black lit a match and peered into her face, but Esther the White pushed her arm away. "Stop that." Esther the Black put out the match. "I'm perfectly rational," Esther the White said. "It's the Demerol that makes me forget."

Esther the Black swung her legs onto the sea wall and held her knees. "All right," she said, "tell me."

Esther the White laughed, but no sound came from her throat. "I thought you didn't want to know."

Esther the Black did not answer, but she waited, and, after a while, her grandmother began again, but she spoke only in English now, and she spoke more slowly, following the thread of time, so that the visit to Dr. Schwartz's office really did happen forty years after she had been in the arms of the tattooed man. And by the time the night was over, and the frogs had stopped their calling, by the time fishermen had begun to push their boats up onto the beach, Esther the Black was beginning to know her grandmother. Esther the White was drowsy, from sleeplessness, from medication. Still she spoke of her life. She spoke in words that were as thin as porcelain, as thick as a stone vase with a circular frieze: around the poured wine, the stored honey, memory had been sculpted.

Soon they could hear the tides grow stronger and watch the morning rise over the harbor. Esther the White untied her scarf and let her hair move in the breeze; Esther the Black smiled and smoked the last cigarette in the pack. From a distance, it would have been nearly impossible, in the shadows, in the pale morning fog, to tell the two women apart.